Monsters In The Park

A Timberhaven Novel

Aaron Conaway

A K&Q Press Publication

Front Cover Art by SageTribe Art

First Edition 2025

Books by Aaron Conaway

The Michael Gideon Collection

Tales for Halloween
Tales for Halloween vol. 2
Tales of the Dark and Strange (Coming Soon!)

New Vision Comics Collective

Harrowed Earth
Book 1 *Appalachian Blues*
Book 2 *Cicero Wants You*
Book 3 *Sordid Deals* (Coming Soon!)

The Timberhaven Chronicles

The Weaver Trilogy
Before The Weaver
Waking The Weaver
Forging The Weaver (Coming Soon!)

The Juniper Soot Trilogy
Monsters In The Park

Table of Contents

For Cody, Kirsten, Alexis, and Lucas

Who grew up faster than Juniper and Jake but have kept their childhood imaginations with which to wonder, create, and dream.

Love, Uncle

And, as always, for Bella

Who loves Juniper Soot above all my creations.

The village of Timberhaven
October 31, 1988
Halloween

Rodger pulled the car over to the side of the street,

checking his mirrors before putting it in Park. A wave of young

trick-or-treaters roamed as far as he could see. He turned to his

young daughter, Melinda, dressed as a princess in the back

seat.

"Okay, kiddo, do you have your flashlight?" Rodger

asked. A group of kids dressed as Ghostbusters went by,

chasing another kid dressed as a ghost.

"Yes, Daddy, I do. Can I get candy now?"

"Yes, yes. Now, you know the routine, right? Up one

side and then down the other, back to me, staying on the

sidewalk at all times except when you cross at Mrs. Swenson's

house, yeah?"

"I *know*, Daddy." The princess moaned, "I will, I promise." Melinda's little hand reached for the door handle as Rodger unbuckled her seatbelt.

"Take it easy," Rodger said. "There's plenty of trick-or-treat time left. Here, don't forget your jack-o-lantern." He passed the orange bucket out to Melinda as she delicately straightened the white frill of her princess-pink dress. "Feels like you've got a ton already!"

"Thank you, Daddy!" Melinda said, grabbing her bucket and making off for the first house on the street, mindful of letting a couple of older kids dressed as Raggedy Ann and Andy pass in front of her.

Rodger smiled as he watched his little girl walk up the sidewalk toward the house. He loved Timberhaven in the autumn and at Halloween most of all. The orange and browns of the oak and cypress moved in time to a gentle wind, the dark purple of smoke bush and deep yellow of Solomon's seal complimenting the affair. It was unseasonably warm, Rodger noted, taking out his book of crosswords as Melinda began walking toward the next house up the street. One really didn't *need* a jacket, Rodger said to himself, agreeing with his earlier assessment of letting Melinda go trick-or-treating without her coat.

"But Daddy," she had said, working Rodger over. He was such a fool for Melinda's *Daddy*. "My coat will wrinkle my gown, and princesses don't have wrinkled gowns. And we can't see breaths. See?" She proceeded to exhale sharply.

And with that, Rodger's princess had gotten to trick-or-treat without her coat.

Melinda waved to him from the porch of the second house as she waited for an answer to her knock, smiling her biggest smile.

Rodger waved back and then looked down at his crossword.

"Michael Knight's co-pilot," Rodger read aloud. "Six across." Rodger had an annoying habit of clicking his pen as he thought on his crossword. Cli-click. Cli-click. Cli-click. Onlookers found it maddening, as evidenced by an unseemly incident at the DMV last year during a two-hour wait. Cli-click. Cli-click. Cli-click.

"K.I.T.T.!" Michael shouted as he wrote in the answer, grinning proudly.

And so it went. Answer after answer, Rodger made his way through the crossword. STAIRWAY followed WIZARD; TEA came after PRESIDENT, on and on until he finished another puzzle and turned the page to start a third.

That was when her absence hit him. When time caught up, and he recognized she should be back by now. Rodger just knew—had a feeling—that something was wrong.

He looked up quickly, eyes darting from one side of the street to the other, distinguishing all the other children on the road between those who weren't his child and those who could be.

"The pink dress," Rodger said, getting out of the car and speaking to nobody and everybody around him, "I should —th-that should be easy to see out here in—kiddo!" he shouted, running down the street.

"Melinda!"

He turned to another group of children. So many damn kids around; why couldn't he see his? "Have you seen my little girl? She's about this tall, brown hair. She's a princess?" He could see he was unnerving them, hysteria creeping into his eyes. The children shook their heads in unison, afraid of the man who was losing his mind. "MELINDA!"

Rodger ran toward the last house he had seen her at, running through yards, jumping bushes.

"Melinda, my little girl, she's a princess. Have you seen Melinda?" he asked everyone, anyone. Could no one help him? He reached the end of the street, Mrs. Swenson's house. He leaped to the porch and pounded on the screen door.

"Mrs. Swenson! Mrs. Swenson!"

"Land's sake, Mr. Foster, I'm here! What's the matter with you?" a woman in her sixties asked through the screen, her mouth slightly open in worry.

"It's Melinda, Mrs. Swenson, my little one. Has she come here yet?"

"Y-yes," Mrs. Swenson answered, removing her glasses as she did. She was staring at a spot behind Rodger.

Rodger spun around to see where she was looking. It caught his eye almost immediately. There in the street, tipped over with candy strewn all around it, was a bucket shaped like a jack-o-lantern. Frantic, Rodger ran, stopping just short of reaching it. He could read the name at the bottom of the jack-o-lantern.

Melinda Foster.

Rodger fell to his knees in the street as a crowd of children and other adults gathered around him. Their hushed whispers and nervous murmuring became something else he had to sort through to find his daughter. But he couldn't find

Melinda; he couldn't *see* her. Rodger could feel something let go inside. He focused on her name, scrawled with a black magic marker on orange plastic in her handwriting, and screamed.

The buzzing of the crowd.

The sirens in the distance.

The colors of autumn.

All muted by a father's anguish.

Safe

In The

Sun

October 2009

Juniper

Juniper Soot aimed a sunbeam through a broken pair of glasses she'd found earlier that day, directing it at an empty two-liter soda bottle in hopes of melting the nozzle off the top. She had seen kids who did something similar to bugs, but the thought of that made Juniper's stomach go wiggly.

Juniper was eight, though she didn't behave as some other eight-year-olds do. She didn't fidget or dance about, and while she daydreamed quite a lot, she rarely played pretend.

Juniper preferred experiments.

She read *everything*. Science was her favorite subject, though she sometimes read history books on the occasional Sunday morning when she had nothing else to read and none of her experiments needed tending.

Mold was Juniper's latest scientific fascination, and she currently had no less than three moldy items (a chunk of cheese, a piece of bread, and her favorite, an old strawberry that had blackened and caved in on itself) tucked away in an old freezer she'd gotten to work in the junkyard.

Juniper *loved* the junkyard, spending every free moment she had within the confines of its fences. She kept a makeshift shed as her laboratory, with all her favorite books tucked away in a broken high school locker she'd dragged inside.

Juniper's parents had died in a car accident in March. Her father had been a singer. Her mother played guitar. When they were alive, her parents sang a song about the sea and its creatures. Her mother also hummed a song to her at bedtime every night, one that Juniper now hummed when she was at her lowest. Those memories made her happy, though Juniper never told anyone about them. She only thought about them when she was sad, and that was a little less often since March—when Juniper was the most miserable that she'd ever been— particularly when she had her focus on experiments.

Juniper lived with her grandmother, Molly, who Juniper thought was *always* sad. Molly didn't speak much to her granddaughter, which caused Juniper to think Molly didn't like having to look after her, so she mostly just tried to stay out of her grandmother's way. She'd tried explaining to Molly once why she needed some baking soda for an experiment, but Molly hadn't understood her. She told Juniper the same thing she often did: "No, honey. You'll hurt yourself."

Molly made a tuna casserole every day. Juniper was reasonably sure it was all she knew how to make, which is why Juniper had taught herself how to use Molly's old microwave. Juniper would cut a piece of bologna into strips and microwave them, then put mustard on them and wrap everything up in a tortilla. It was her favorite. Molly stuck to the casserole.

It's not that Juniper disliked her grandmother; she just didn't understand why Molly always cried. Juniper cried, sure, but not all of the time.

She read instead.

In fact, that was Juniper's favorite thing about living with Molly—their weekly trips to the library. Molly let Juniper check out absolutely anything she wanted. Francine, the librarian, found it strange that Juniper rarely, if ever, checked out books more attuned to her age group or, at the very least, fairytales, but Molly would tell her, "The child loves reading. What more could I ask for?" Francine would "tsk" and leave it at that.

The truth was that Juniper got enough of fairytales in her real, everyday life. Why would she want to read more about what she saw all the time? Maybe she didn't see actual fairies or trolls or anything, but she lived in Timberhaven, and she hadn't had to live there very long before she realized that magical, strange things happened all around her.

Even before she met Story.

Story was a brown tabby cat that Juniper had befriended during the summer. While Juniper knew that most cats don't talk, she couldn't argue that Story did. At least, she spoke to Juniper. She didn't know if Story talked to anybody else, but she'd never seen her doing so.

As if summoned, Story came from around the corner, casually swishing her tail as she walked up and nuzzled Juniper's leg. Juniper continued to focus on the sunbeam.

"I think it's about to melt," Juniper whispered to Story excitedly.

Story peered at the bottle.

"I believe you're right." the tabby said through a yawn.

"Isn't it neat?"

"Certainly." Story said, making her way over to a tractor tire tipped on its side.

Just then, the plastic peeled back around a small hole, folding the nozzle sideways. Juniper smiled a great big smile.

"It worked! I love a successful experiment," she admitted, meeting Story at the tractor tire. She put the glasses in the pocket of her sweatshirt, a heavy thing that was two sizes too big for her, but it had a microscope embroidered on it, so of course, it was Juniper's favorite thing to wear. "Why are you so tired?"

Story stretched out and collapsed.

"Well, I've just gotten back from a long journey, Juniper, and daresay, I'm in need of a catnap."

Juniper chuckled at the pun. "That's the only kind of nap you take, Story." Her smile sagged softly to a puzzled look. "Hey, I thought you weren't going to go on any more adventures without me."

"This wasn't an adventure, Juniper. I was getting information. A rather boring trip, actually, just one that was very far away."

"Ooo," Juniper clapped excitedly. "A new story?"

"Of a kind," the cat replied, hinting like one with a secret but won't share it. "But this isn't meant for you. Not yet, anyway." She added quickly when Juniper's face fell.

"Oh, all right." Juniper knew that, for whatever reason, there were some tales that Story couldn't share until certain things had happened. She always got around to telling Juniper the outstanding ones eventually, but she couldn't break the rules.

"Wanna look for pennies? We could go get mints and soda at the gas station." Juniper tried changing the subject.

"Not just now, sorry. I think I will sleep for a little while. Besides, it's Saturday! Haven't you got a package coming today?"

Juniper jumped up, taking the eyeglasses from her pocket and placing them back in her laboratory. "I forgot! Okay, I'll come back later, Story. Bye!" And she ran for home, desperately hoping the mailman had already been by the house and that a brown box would be waiting for her on the porch.

Slow

Winslow "Slow" Perkins had an overnight bag slung over his shoulder and his guitar case held carefully before him as he stepped off the bus. Timberhaven. It had taken a lot of doing, but he finally was here.

Well, Grandma, I made it here, he thought to himself. A memory of sitting on his Grandma's porch back in Florence, Kentucky, popped into his mind's eye: it was summertime five or six years back, and the two of them were making lemonade in a glass pitcher on a wooden tray. The white of her apron was bright in his memory against her dark skin. She'd started humming a tune he hadn't heard from her before.

"What's that song, grandma?" he'd asked, stirring the sugar into the pitcher.

"Hmm?" She grinned, slicing lemons. "Oh, that's one from back in my day. You keep up with your guitar, and maybe I'll teach it to you someday."

"Did you sing it in Timberhaven?" the little boy version of him had asked.

His grandma's grin had turned into a glowing smile, and she sort of stared off into the horizon. "Sure did spark something in you, telling about Timberhaven, haven't I?" She laughed and wiped off the tray with her apron, Slow having spilled some lemonade due to overzealous stirring. "Oh, I guess I did at that. Long before I met your grandpa, this would've been when I sang with Charlie Ditchwater and John Sugars—well, none of us used our real names back then, but stage names, you understand? Anyhow, our trio had heard-tell of a smoky bar in this little midwest town where you could find songs—just snap 'em out of the air! And that all the greats had been there, too. Just about anybody you ever heard of."

A year or so after that day, Slow's grandma got sick. A few years later, Slow had found himself standing in the very town his grandma had been in when she was barely older than he was now.

Timberhaven.

"Time to find some of that magic," Slow said aloud. He lowered his guitar case to his side and began walking toward a bulletin board, hoping for some small direction to this bar he'd heard so much about.

Juniper

The mailman hadn't, in fact, delivered the mail by the time Juniper got home. She sat on the front porch steps with her face in her hands, holding her head by her cheeks. It was a rough day to be an eight-year-old, bound to the authority and timetable of adults as she was. Juniper continuously popped her head over her grandmother's shrubs to try and catch the mailman coming, figuring on running to meet him if he had her package, only to return to her mopey perch when he wasn't there.

It had taken three months of penny-collecting and a birthday to save for it, and then two weeks of begging Molly to use her credit card online and mail off for it after that, but it would all be worth it once Juniper got the kit to make her very own miniature Tesla coil. It would tie her Nikola Tesla costume entirely together for her school's upcoming Halloween costume party. She already had the wig and fake mustache, and Molly had a bunch of old clothes upstairs in the attic where Juniper found the perfect suit.

All she needed was the coil and a boy's dress shirt, and she'd be ready for Halloween.

If the mailman would only arrive.

"Maybe he is stuck in a ditch," Juniper pondered. "With a great big log rolled onto his leg that a bear pushed over accidentally while it was trying to get honeycombs from an old beehive. And he doesn't dare shout out for help on account of the bear being right there lapping up honey, and the bees are buzzing about, sensing his fear of the bear and of them, and he's worried that they are looking to sting him." She hopped back up and looked worriedly down the road.

"Poor guy. He's probably trying his hardest to get here with my package, hardly any concern about his self." She squinted as hard as she could but still didn't see the mailman coming.

While Juniper maybe didn't pretend very often, she could undoubtedly follow a line of thought to its seemingly inevitable conclusion. Even when that conclusion involved hungry bears and angry bees.

Juniper heard a rustling behind her. Spinning, she caught Jake Steadherd peeking through the bushes at her, his great big googly eyes too large for his six-year-old head.

"Jake, what are you doing? Can't you see I'm busy waiting for the mailman?"

Jake came out from behind the bushes, looking at his feet.

"I wasn't doin' nothin' wrong," he told her, albeit guiltily. "Just seein' what you was doin'."

Juniper had met Jake earlier that year on the playground at school. A bigger kid was teasing Jake about his eyes, and the teasing had turned to the bigger kid and his friends pitching rocks at Jake. Not at all unfamiliar with being bullied, Juniper had seen fit to help Jake by running up and telling him that his teacher was looking for him. It wasn't true, of course, since Juniper didn't even know who Jake's teacher *was*, but it made everyone scatter regardless. (Juniper wasn't one to stand up to bullies so much as outmaneuver them.)

Jake had never had anyone look out for him before that day and would now occasionally show up at her house to see what she was doing.

"Well, like I said, Jake," she said, talking more slowly to him without meaning to. "I'm waiting for the mailman. He's bringing me a package I ordered special for the Halloween party at school. He should be here already, but I think we can forgive him being late, what with the bear and bees and everything."

Jake's eyes went wide, and he hid behind Juniper. He looked down the street and wondered if that dark patch behind the tree line in Mrs. Willis' backyard was a giant bear stalking him and Juniper after having eaten the mailman in a gulp.

"Jake," Juniper asked behind her shoulder. "What are *you* doing?"

"Shh! I'm hiding from the bear." Jake whispered.

"Jake!" a voice yelled from the street.

Juniper and Jake jumped. Three boys rode their bikes and skidded sideways into Juniper's yard. The biggest of them, Tod, was Jake's older brother, and if there was a wickeder boy in all of Timberhaven, Juniper didn't know who he was. At fifteen, Tod had already been in more trouble than any three adults Juniper knew. His friends were each a year younger than him. Curtis was a huge, husky kid. He gave a toady little laugh at anything Tod said as if it was the highest quality of humor. Bobby was the third. He was quiet, with dead eyes.

These three boys were the entirety of the reason why Juniper distrusted teenagers across the board.

"I wasn't doin' nothin'—" Jake began his standby line.

"Shut it," his brother interrupted. "Get home, now, before I bounce a rock off your melon, Owl Eyes."

Curtis snickered.

Jake, having forgotten all about Juniper's bear at the sight of something he feared more, ran toward home without so much as a goodbye glance at Juniper. He pulled his too-big pants up high as he ran away.

Tod turned his attention to Juniper. He smiled a mean, toothy smile.

"What's up, Junkyard?" he asked her, causing Curtis to snicker again. "Where's your grandma?"

Juniper took a step back up toward her front door. "Sh-she's inside," she said, looking around, silently pleading for *anyone* to come along.

"You haven't ever told nobody nothin' about us, right, Junkyard?" Tod asked, setting his bike down. "Remember what we said would happen." He stepped over his bike toward Juniper, moving like a big cat hunting prey. "Do you need another lesson?"

"A reminder, I think," Curtis said, snickering at what he saw as wit and dropping his bike to the ground, too.

"Let's be quick, guys." was all Bobby said.

Juniper ran onto the porch and around the side, hopping over the railing as fast as she could. She ran down the side yard and into the woods between her house and Mr. Boyer's next door, not daring to look back to see if the boys were following. She could hear their heavy feet running after her, tearing through the leaves and underbrush. Juniper grabbed a thin, low-hanging branch as she ran and let it go, snapping it back into place behind her.

"Ow! Stupid little witch!" Curtis yelled.

Juniper blasted through the tree line and out into Mr. Boyer's yard, praying that he was outside working. She didn't figure they would keep chasing her then.

Her little legs began to hurt.

"Over here!" Bobby shouted to the others. He'd stayed on his bike and was pedaling fast, bearing down on her from the street like a homing missile. Juniper pivoted away from him and ran again as fast as she could, crossing the street toward Kings Park.

I can make it, she thought. *Only four streets down. I can make it.* She dared a look behind her. Bobby was coming fast, and Tod and Curtis had gone back for their bikes, too. Juniper's legs were burning, her little muscles pushed to their limit.

The boys on their bikes came closer still.

Juniper realized she wouldn't reach the park before they got to her. She needed a new plan. As she rounded the Pavilion —a giant, metal shed home to swap meets on the weekends— Juniper noticed that a side door was open. She veered and ducked inside, feeling as though her heart would explode.

"Hello?" she yelled, hoping that someone was right there—someone she could use to deflect the attention of Tod and his thugs. But nobody answered her. Juniper could hear the boys dropping their bikes outside. She dove under a table of hoodies and sweaters to hide.

"She's in here someplace," Bobby said.

"Juuunkyaard…" Tod whispered, insomuch as a Rottweiler might whisper.

Juniper put her head between her knees. She was sure that they could hear her pounding heart, her oxygen-starved lungs causing her to gulp air.

Just go away, just go away, just go away. Juniper thought the mantra again and again.

A garage door to the side of the Pavilion started opening automatically.

"Tod, let's get out of here; someone's coming!" Bobby whispered.

"Fine," Tod whispered. "You're lucky, Junkyard—this time. We'll be lookin' for you. That's a promise."

"You can't stay in here forever!" Curtis yelled, laughing as they went out the door.

And with that, the boys left.

Juniper collapsed on the floor under the table, her chest still rising and falling rapidly. She'd never run so hard in her life. A stitch started on her side from the effort.

"I don't know what that was about," a voice from the shadows across from Juniper said. "But you looked like you could use a friend."

Jake

Jake was supposed to go home. Tod had said so, and Jake was very afraid of his older brother and the yardstick his brother called his Corrector. It was wrapped in duct tape on one end so Tod could grip it, wielding it like a sword. The other end had thumbtacks pushed through it, perfect for gouging Jake. His back had just healed from all the damage done over a month ago (Jake had made the mistake of eating a Pop-Tart that his brother had wanted) by Tod and his Corrector.

Jake knew he was to go home, but something along the way had distracted him. He heard something moving out there in the trees, following him. At first, Jake thought it was the bear again, out to eat him. But he couldn't see any bear, and the moving noises he heard were slighter than Jake figured a bear might make.

Scared of nearly everything by nature, Jake made to run home again. But that's when he saw it. Or rather, saw its teeth gleaming at him from the dark between the trees. Sharp, crooked, jagged things; flashes of silver glistening through the filth of its mouth. It snorted, whatever it was, and seemed to Jake like it was about to charge. Jake ran as though the devil himself was chasing him, taking off just as the creature did.

He'd made it about twenty feet when his pants fell around his ankles. To be fair, they were Tod's old hand-me-downs and had probably been handed down before Jake was of a size to use them, but there he was, just the same, sprawled out with his underwear showing as the thing with the dirty silver teeth came for him.

A horn blared at Jake. As though waking from a daze, he looked from the car back to where the creature had been, but it was gone. No teeth anywhere.

"Get out of the road!" the man driving the car yelled as he swerved to Jake's right and drove away. "Darn kids!" he added.

Jake got to his feet and pulled his pants back up, holding them up snugly with one hand, the other keeping the sun from his eyes while he searched the woods. Nothing. He didn't see the creature anywhere. He ran for home anyway.

"I'll draw that monster," he thought. "And I'll tell Juniper about it, and she'll have a trick to catch it, and we'll be rich and not live with Tod no more." Which typically was what Jake daydreamed. Not necessarily about drawing monsters or being rich but about living with Juniper in her house with her grandma and playing in the junkyard with her.

And not living with Tod anymore.

Jake heard a low growl coming from behind him. He ran faster. The growl grew louder. Jake thought he could feel hot breath on his neck. He started to cry. Jake's mom had never really been warm to him, and he didn't really remember his dad, so when he cried, it wasn't for his parents.

He wished Juniper was with him now. She'd know what to do.

The growling sounded angrier.

Hungrier.

Timberhaven

The piper spun, circling her drummer and fiddler in a ripple of orange and brown fabric as the trio played an Irish jig. She danced to the music, feeling the rhythm in her blood. Onlookers were swept away by her, clapping their hands in merriment and searching their pockets for money to give. The piper smiled behind her pipe as she and her bandmates' hat began to fill with loose change, even a dollar or two.

"That's a lovely tune!" a familiar voice called from the crowd.

The piper placed the voice to the face it belonged to.

"Emmett!" she yelled, abruptly ending the band's tune.

A tall, thin, leather-skinned man emerged from the crowd, a banjo slung over his shoulder. He took his hat off to the piper, the gray of his hair and the wrinkles around his eyes the only things betraying his years. The piper embraced him in a hug.

"Vi, girl, how are you?" he asked once the embrace ended.

"Fantastic! It's fall in Timberhaven, after all." She smiled, "We didn't know if you were going to make it this weekend or not. I'm so happy you did!"

Emmett nodded hellos to the other members of Vi's band. He brought his banjo around in front of him.

"Of course I did! Weren't gonna miss the Mushroom Festival, was I? I hopped a bus from Louisville as soon as I had the ticket cost worked out." He picked a few notes on the banjo.

Seeing their crowd of onlookers dispersing, Vi signaled to the others, and the newly formed foursome began a bluegrass tune.

The people returned to crowd around, cheering as one song led to the next, the music of the Appalachians speaking to them and coaxing out their coin, laughing and dancing around the street performers all the while.

Their next song, the third, started strong, born as it was of mountains and mines, but then Emmett began to fade his banjo playing out. Slowly, at first, his face full of confusion, as though he was performing a song that wasn't meshing with what the others played until he finally stopped playing altogether. He hugged his banjo, his most prized possession, close, and peered into and beyond the crowd around them. Vi drew her pipe from her lips.

"Emmett?" she asked worriedly, fearful that the old man was having an attack of some form or another. She noticed as his hands trembled around the base and neck of his banjo. He shook his head at her.

"N-no, I…" he stuttered. "I don't reckon I will at that." He told her, gathering what few things he had.

"Emmett, what is it?" the fiddle player rose to meet Emmett's gaze.

"The music's gone wrong." Emmett whispered, "Timberhaven…s'not right. The music here—it…"

Nearly as one, the crowd gasped as Emmett, the banjo player from Kentucky, collapsed to the ground.

Molly

Molly started to heat the water on the stove for the third time. However, just like the first two times she'd tried, when she placed the pot filled with water onto the burner, an immense sadness would force her to remove it again. A grief that was very real to her, incredibly vivid, though without origin. It was almost the exact pain and sorrow she'd felt when she'd gotten word that Alice, her daughter and Juniper's mother, and Gene, Juniper's father, had died in the car accident. Only, it *wasn't* the same.

It was like having someone else's idea of what that pain felt like, their impression of it, drilled into her brain, but it only happened at intervals. Like when one rides a merry-go-round, and their eyes fix on one object each time they come around—a tree or car or color—and for that brief moment that they're spinning past, it's the only thing in the world that they can see.

And, just like on the first two attempts, Molly began to cry in hopeless despair. Then she'd take the pot, dump out the water, and set the pot down on the counter, and the feeling would disappear as though it had never happened.

The stove wasn't the only place it happened to Molly, either. Specific actions at any time and place would mean the same results. Anguished sobbing, confusion, and then back to normal. Her brain would click back and work as though her own again.

"Come on, Molly girl," she said aloud, grabbing a dish towel to dry off the pot. "You're losing it."

She didn't know what that would mean for poor Juniper, and that worried her more than anything. The child had already lost so much in her young life. Molly knew that Juniper didn't like it, living here with her, but at least Molly was family. She loved the girl, whether Juniper liked her or not, but Molly didn't know how to relate to Juniper. The child was so incredibly smart, always building this or that and all of her little tests. Molly spent half the day worried sick that Juniper would blow herself up, and the other half worried that Juniper would end up in a home someplace if Molly were losing it.

So, Molly didn't tell anyone about the sadness. She just stayed in the house as much as possible and tried to muddle through. Get a handle on things.

Like how to heat water in a pot.

Rodger

November 2, 1988

Rodger stopped writing long enough to light a fresh cigarette off the dying cherry of his spent one, his hands twitching from sleep deprivation. Half-empty chicken buckets and burger wrappers covered the dinner table in front of him. Ashley, his wife of nearly ten years, stared out the kitchen window, absently wiping the countertops as she cried silently.

Have You Seen Me? was handwritten across the top of the flyer in thick black magic marker. Rodger finished writing their phone number along the bottom. A Polaroid snapshot of Melinda—from her birthday last year. She was smiling, holding up her princess cake—was taped into the middle of the flyer.

Juniper

"Who are you?" Juniper asked from her hiding spot. The voice from above her sounded like it belonged to a big kid, and one never knew what big kids were going to do.

"Winslow," said the boy, "but my friends call me Slow."

Juniper stayed put, but her curiosity got the better of her until she asked, "What are you doing here? Do you live here?"

Slow laughed. "Nah, it ain't like that." He explained. "I just got to Timberhaven. My grandma…she used to visit here. Anyhow, a guy in town told me I might be able to get a shower up here, maybe find some guitar strings. So, what's your name? Do *you* live under *there*?"

Slow offered down his hand, and Juniper tentatively put her small hand into his big one, climbing out from under the table. "My name is Juniper." While typically distrustful of any teens, Slow *had* just gotten her away from Tod, and something about how he'd mentioned his grandma reminded Juniper of a small, worried spot inside herself. She decided to trust Slow.

"Why do your friends call you slow? Can you not run very fast?"

Slow smiled, "No, it's a nickname. Short for Win*Slow*. Juniper's a cool name, though," Slow said, walking back to his bag in the corner. "So why were those guys chasing after you?"

"They're just stupid bullies," Juniper told him, looking to change the subject. She noticed Slow's guitar case. "Is there a guitar in there? Can you play it?"

"Sure can." Slow beamed. "I'm a bluesman."

"A man?" Juniper said without thinking. "You don't look old enough."

Slow laughed again. "You're funny. Just say whatever pops into your head. I like that." He told her, smiling. "Nah, not quite sixteen yet. What I meant is that I'm a blues guitar player."

Juniper had heard of Blues music, had listened with a tilted head to try and hear it coming up from Old Town, a section on the other side of Timberhaven. Juniper wasn't allowed to go, per Molly's instructions, and so desperately wanted to. The junkyard was as far toward the direction of Old Town as she was allowed, and from there, she could sometimes hear the sounds of Old Town wafting up to her invitingly, serving as Juniper's very own Mangiafuoco, made of scents and song.

"Can I hear you play?" Juniper asked.

"What, here? Now?" Slow slung his bag over his shoulder and picked his guitar case back up, the look of excitement coming across his face that every born entertainer gets after an invite to perform. "I dunno, those three guys seemed pretty intense."

Juniper looked out the door that Tod and his friends had used. "Oh, yeah, them. Thanks for distracting them with the garage door."

"No problem. So where ya headed, Juniper?" He pushed the button to close the automatic garage door and then started them walking back out the side door. Juniper thought maybe not all teenagers were terrible.

"Well, I was waiting for the mailman. He's supposed to bring me a Tesla coil." Juniper explained.

"Tesla, eh?" Slow locked the door behind them. "You some kinda scientist?"

While talking over adventures with Story was a close second, there was nothing in the world that Juniper loved to talk about more than science. She had just started third grade, but Juniper had bought an old eighth-grade Science book at her previous school's yearly book sale last year. It was missing a few pages in the fossil section and one page at the end of a description of energy transference (causing Juniper to figure out how photosynthesis worked on her own), but it was still one of Juniper's favorite treasures.

"Not a real one yet, but I will be when I grow up." She told Slow proudly as the two of them walked. "I do all kinds of experiments and tests in my laboratory. Do you know what mold is?"

Slow grinned. "Sure. The green stuff that grows on old bread, right?"

Juniper's eyes went wide. "I *have* some on bread!" she exclaimed. She thought Slow might, *maybe*, be okay. For a big kid. "Isn't it amazing?"

Slow

Slow was getting a kick out of this strange little girl, talking a mile a minute about energy and the sun and mold. It was like he was playing catch-up after missing a year's worth of Science in school. Back when Slow had attended school. He'd dropped out, and left home four months back, determined to take his guitar playing on the road and make it as a bluesman.

He just hadn't counted on being so hungry all the time. Busking didn't pay nearly as well outside of the bigger cities, but he'd finally made it to Timberhaven. Timberhaven was where the secret to the music was, or so he'd grown up hearing from his grandma. The key to all of his dreams could be just around the corner.

Slow and Juniper came into a park under a big metal signpost that read *Kings Park* in iron letters artistically crafted with little iron birds around them. There was a crown between the words Kings and Park that had red glass in place to look like rubies. The grass was immaculate, thick like shag carpet but cropped close. As they walked, Slow and Juniper crossed a chess set topiary with detailed bushes standing three feet high, trimmed to look like chess pieces, all save the Kings, which were statues made of bronze.

"This park is amazing," Slow said, accidentally interrupting Juniper's science talk in his appreciation of their surroundings.

"What? Oh, yeah, Kings Park is neat." Juniper agreed, sounding to Slow like someone who was used to people getting sick of talking about science long before she did.

"Why is it called Kings Park?" Slow asked.

"Well," Juniper began. "Some adults say that it's named for a rich family who lived here in town, the Kings, but the real reason is much better."

"So what's the real reason?" Slow asked, studying a bush shaped like a knight.

"Um…I'm not sure you'd believe me." Juniper said, inspecting a rock she'd accidentally kicked, flipping it over in search of fossils.

"Try me." He said, turning to her.

"Okay, I guess," Juniper stood back up, leaving the rock since there hadn't been any fossils. "But you can't stop being my friend if you think it's freaky. Other kids do that all of the time, but since you're a big kid, you shouldn't. Deal?"

Slow was sure that Juniper was the most fun person he'd ever met in all his fifteen years.

"You got it, Juniper, deal."

"This park was built in celebration of the kings of old. The Ogre Kings and Fairy Kings. The kings of Man and Serpent, Hound, and Sea; for every king that ever was and ever will be." Juniper finished with a bow and a flourish of her little hands.

Slow sat his guitar case down and clapped his hands.

"Bravo!" he cheered to Juniper. "That was great, kiddo. Did you memorize that from somewhere?" he asked, recognizing a performance when he saw one.

"That was just how my friend Story told it to me." Juniper smiled.

"Salutations upon our meeting at cross promenades, Ms. Soot!" said a man in a patched purple suit and dirty bowler hat, sitting on a little bench beside the chess topiary. "And how does this splendorous Saturday find you?" The man stood from the bench with a bow, asking the last with a tip of his hat.

Juniper

"Hello, Mr. Jack!" Juniper responded happily. "I am having a very good day now. I've made a new friend." She pointed to Slow.

"Indeed?" Mr. Jack said, coming over. "I must shake this gentleman's hand, then, eh, how is it you are called?"

Slow reluctantly shook Mr. Jack's hand, speaking through closed teeth. "Winslow." Juniper thought that Slow seemed to have the inherent distrust of adults that Juniper usually had with teenagers.

"Winslow!" Mr. Jack yelled. "Wonderful name, stupendous! Well, you mustn't let me keep you, children, but must carry on whence you were going." As he made to leave, however, he looked back to Juniper. "I'm the part of the bird that's not in the sky. I can swim in the ocean and yet remain dry. What am I?"

Slow turned to Juniper. "Um, what?"

"It's a riddle," Juniper said, turning to Mr. Jack. "Part of the bird, not in the sky…swims in the ocean but stays dry, hmmm." She turned the puzzle over and over while Mr. Jack hummed a happy tune, waiting.

"A shadow!" she yelled, finally.

"Right, you are, my precocious pal, right indeed. See you later!" Mr. Jack kicked up his heels and walked away, humming his tune.

"That guy is weird," Slow said once Mr. Jack was out of earshot.

Juniper looked at Slow. "I don't think he's weird. He just knows a lot of words and riddles, stuff like that."

"Whatever you say, kiddo," Slow picked up his guitar case again.

Juniper didn't know how she felt about being called kiddo, but she liked that Slow hadn't made fun of her for sharing her story about Kings Park. He didn't tell her he wouldn't be her friend anymore either, which made her happy, too. Juniper found it challenging to make friends (except for Story, she had been easy), and, while she was okay with making a friend and then having that friend seem to change their mind about her, Juniper wasn't ready to have that happen with Slow. She hadn't even gotten to know about bluesmen yet.

Just as she was about to ask Slow some questions about the blues, a small voice called from behind the topiary bishop.

"Juniper! C'mere, quick!" Jake whispered. Though, it was as much a whisper as one does when they drop something very heavy on their pinky toe.

"Jake?" Juniper asked, peering into the bishop. "What are you doing here? I just had to run away from your dumb brother and his friends! If Slow hadn't—why aren't you wearing pants?" she laughed, covering her mouth with her hands.

Jake came from behind the topiary in just his shirt and underwear, seeming to have forgotten that he was half-naked.

"I came to find you and tell you about the monster!" Jake explained, then, suddenly remembering his current situation, tried to cover himself behind the topiary again. He looked up at Slow. "I'm Jake. Who are you?"

Slow bristled a little. "Name's Slow, little man."

"What monster are you talking about?" Juniper asked.

"I dunno what it is, but it's got teeth and—buncha squiggly arms with hands on the end of some and feet on other ones and teeth, and he eats pants 'cause he ate mine when he tried to eat me, and Tod's gonna kill me when I come home with no pants," Jake explained in a breath. "Can we draw the monster? And then you catch it, maybe this slow kid," he pointed to Slow, "will help, and we can be rich and buy a whole lot of stuff and new bikes."

"Are you sure you didn't just get your pants dirty, and now you're telling fibs? Story told me that monsters can't come into New Town." Juniper said.

Timberhaven was a centuries-old town, and it was mostly split into two halves; New Town and Old Town. New Town, where Juniper and Jake lived and Kings Park was, is where most of the restorations, additional buildings, and newer housing were being built. The interstate exit was there, and, as a result, so were the fast-food chains and the gas stations. Old Town, on the other hand, was where the residents who wanted to keep Timberhaven as it always had been lived. Cell phones, internet connection, these things rarely, if ever, worked in Old Town. It's also where the Village was, the tightly-knit group of artists and musicians, poets, and artisans who sold their goods from colorful tents and booths. Juniper thought it sounded like heaven. But Old Town had a dark side, too, which is why Molly wouldn't let Juniper go until she was older. Juniper had heard lots of different stories. Like that ghosts lived in the woods in Old Town and that some people could play a song that made you forget who you were.

And that Old Town is where the monsters live.

"But I wasn't *in* Old Town!" Jake promised. "I was heading home like Tod said to. And then in the woods there by old Mr. Boyer's house, by that old gnarly tree, there was a monster!"

"Take it easy, kid," Slow interjected. "Slow down. Juniper, what's he talking about?"

"I don't know for sure. Let's go back to my house. I think I have some old pants that Jake can wear, and I'll get out some paper and pencils." Juniper planned.

"You two go ahead," Slow said doubtfully. "I'll catch up with you another time. I've gotta go see about playing a little, try to make some money for dinner."

Juniper stopped. "You don't want to come?"

"Don't worry, kiddo," Slow pointed to a spot at the edge of Kings Park. "I'll be right over in that corner if you have any more trouble with those boys. Okay?"

"Yeah, okay," Juniper moped as Slow walked to his corner. She wanted to listen to him play guitar and to ask him all about the blues, but Jake didn't have any pants on, and he was bound to get killed when he got home. Plus, she thought Jake seemed kind of sincere about the monster he said he saw.

"Okay, Jake, let's go get you some clothes," the two started to walk back toward Juniper's house. "So, how big were these teeth?"

Timberhaven

The creature, Claptrap—an oddity of discarded body parts, too many hands growing from multiple armpits, and four spindly arms springing from the toothy maw at his center—had been lost for decades amongst the verge of human ideas, dreams, and scattered thoughts, as monsters will do.

A 29-year-old electric lineman named Kent, there on his lunch break, stood in a circle with people from various walks of life, sharing stories each had made up.

Claptrap had a purpose on this side of reality—a job, a mission he was meant to accomplish. However, the ability to focus was not strong in most Pitchborn, and for Claptrap, even less so.

The woman next to Kent, Tess, had told one about a tax accountant who spent her evenings liberating babies' dreams from dark pageants. A ghastly, twisting story that all gathered had enjoyed but which now made Kent nervous to begin his own. Yet still, he did. "Once upon a time,"

It was as blood in the water to Claptrap, whose skin,
like unformed clay, bristled with gooseflesh.

Having been formed with all teeth and no eyes,
Claptrap knew nothing of this new storyteller besides his being
set apart from Claptrap. That, being born of this world, Kent
was drawn to the moon. Loved by the sun.

And Claptrap hated him for it, even at the expense of
his mission.

Molly

Molly wasn't sure how long she'd been standing there, looking at the calendar. She had blanked on it, staring at the red circle around the 31st—Halloween—and Juniper's handwritten note that read *Juniper's School Costume Party* and *Juniper Needs a Boy's White Dress Shirt* written underneath that, with a Post-it on the 30th that read *It's for the costume* and an arrow pointing to her note on the 31st.

Molly had thought it was cute the first time she had read it. She didn't know why, though, that she had lost herself in thought looking at it now. She jumped when she heard a knock at the front door.

Walking to it, she looked out and saw the mailman.

"Hey, Henry," she said, opening the door. "How's the route today?"

"Not bad at all, Molly," the mailman said with a smile. "Got a package here for your little one. I imagine she's been excited for it to arrive."

Molly looked at the box. She had no idea what it was.

"That's for Juniper?" she asked, eyeing the package and turning it around in her hands suspiciously.

Henry looked at the package, pointing at Juniper's name.

"See?" he said. "What, you didn't know she ordered something?"

Molly shook her head. "Who knows with that girl. Kids nowadays, ordering with a click of the mouse."

Henry smiled. "Yeah, they've got it made. Have a good one, Molly," he said with a wave, continuing on his route.

Molly looked at the package some more. She was struggling with a half-remembered notion that she *had* ordered something for Juniper or had been there when Juniper ordered it. Why was it so hard to remember? She put the package on the kitchen table and went to the refrigerator to get something to make sandwiches. It was lunchtime soon, and clearly, Molly wasn't going to be able to make Juniper any macaroni and

cheese with no way to boil the water.

Rodger

December 8, 1988

Rodger gave a brief shiver as he sat at the edge of the sidewalk, hugging his legs in front of him and peering over his knees at the street.

At *that* spot in the street.

It had been over a month, yet the police had no leads as to where Melinda was or who might have taken her. She was just gone. That was the end of their list once they'd ruled Ashley and Rodger out as suspects. Ashley had shut down. She hardly ate, didn't sleep. Rodger couldn't remember the last time she'd talked to him.

Not that he was faring any better.

Rodger had no idea how long he'd been sitting there when he felt someone touch his shoulder, causing him to jump.

"Sorry to startle you, Mr. Foster," Mrs. Swenson began, her eyes wide and sad.

Rodger looked around to discover that the afternoon sun's shift had ended long ago.

"It's, no, it's fine, Mrs. Swenson," he said, getting to his feet. "I've been too long." He brushed his hand through his unkempt hair. "I'll, um, I'll just be going home now."

Rodger hadn't taken three steps before Mrs. Swenson grabbed his arm to stop him.

"I have a sister over in Boulder," she said, turning in front of Rodger, her hand shaking as she spoke. "And sometimes, well, sometimes she has these dreams."

"Dreams," Rodger muttered, half-hearing.

"Now, look, I don't want to go getting your hopes up," Mrs. Swenson admitted.

"What kind of dreams?" Rodger asked, finally paying attention.

"Some say it's hoo-hah," Mrs. Swenson began. "But I know better. I've seen what happens when my sister has one of her dreams and—"

"Mrs. Swenson!" Rodger shouted, making her jump in turn.

"She knows, Rodger," Mrs. Swenson said, regaining her composure. "She's seen where your little girl is."

Jake

Jake pulled the pants up, eyeing with disdain the embroidered flowers that ran up the side of them.

"These are girl pants!" he grumbled.

"Well, duh," Juniper said. "What'd you think I had? I'm a girl!"

"I don't wanna wear no girl's pants!" Jake fussed.

"Well, then I guess you'd better run on home in your underwear," Juniper told him, putting down the paper and pencil she had gotten from the drawing room. "But first, you draw what you saw."

Jake pulled the pants up again, deciding that girl pants were better than no pants.

"No, no, I'll wear 'em home and then take 'em off really fast when I can put my own pants on."

"Okay, but draw first." Juniper pointed impatiently. "What did it look like other than having teeth?"

Jake sat down to draw. He was good at drawing. Tod

usually found his drawings at home and tore them up, but Jake didn't mind. He would redraw anything that had gotten torn up. Jake started with the head but then had to erase it and start over because the monster hadn't had a head, not really, so that was wrong. He had to get it right for Juniper, or else she wouldn't believe him.

"Its body kind of *was* a head, like this here," he said, narrating. "Because that's where its big mouth is. And it had more teeth than this, but I told you a bunch about the teeth already."

What he'd drawn was nothing that came from the real world; its body didn't make sense enough to have been born of Earth. It had no eyes but had what looked like an ear on top of its bald body-head and one where its kind of chin was. And the teeth. So many teeth. Jake was finishing up by putting in its two spindly legs, twice as long as the rest of it, coming out the side of its teardrop-in-reverse-shaped core with elbow-like knees and clawed hands for feet.

"It doesn't have proper arms?" Juniper asked. "Or, are *these* arms, and it hasn't got legs?" she pointed.

"Well, I think these are its arms *and* legs, it used them as both, but it may have had some behind its back," Jake said, adding, "I didn't see back there."

Jake watched Juniper as she looked at his drawing. Her scrunched-up face meant that she was wondering. He put the pencil down and fidgeted with the flower on his borrowed pants some more.

"Juniper?" he finally asked when she was quiet for what he thought was too long. "You believe me, don't you?"

Juniper didn't answer right away. She picked up his drawing and looked closer at it.

"I don't know, Jake," she said with a sigh. "It doesn't look much like anything I've ever heard of."

"Because it's a monster!" Jake exclaimed, looking up in an exasperated effort to find a way to explain things more clearly. "It eats pants and gets boys like me in trouble." This made Jake remember what Tod had said about getting home and how that had happened what seemed like a very long time ago. "I've gotta go, Juniper. I'm gonna get it as it is."

"Alright, I'll keep this here." She said, rolling up his drawing, "No sense in you having to draw it again later if Tod finds it and tears it up." Juniper opened the door to her bedroom and looked to see if Molly was in sight. When she saw that she wasn't, Juniper pushed the door open all the way. "Maybe Tod hasn't gotten home yet. If you run, you may be okay."

Jake started down the hall but turned back to Juniper.

"Juniper," he said really quietly. "I swear, it's real."

Juniper thought it over for a second.

"Okay," she whispered back. "I believe you. Be careful going home."

Timberhaven

The gray-haired barkeep, Gerald Nelson, lit the thick, black candles to the last window in his place. Few in town could understand why a bar had so many candles around, but Gerald was nobody's fool.

He kept track of who owed what tab at his place, The Pub, and never let things get out of hand. Give a guy a little leeway, sure, no need for unpleasantness, and a man needs a drink now and again so far as he was concerned, but you keep an eye out. Mind your Ps and Qs, as his old man had been fond of saying.

So when Unser and Port, two buddies from Gerald's stint in the army, had come busting into his joint all out of breath, Gerald paid attention.

"What's this now, fellas?" Gerald asked, setting up two shot glasses for his friends and reaching for the scotch.

"Gerry, you won't believe it," started Unser through his thick New England accent, "Banjo Emmett just up and died out on the street."

"Mid-song, too," Port added, grabbing the shot in his big, beefy hands and downing it.

"Good Christ, really?" Gerald said, leaning on the bar. "Old Emmett weren't much older than us. His heart, ya think?"

Unser finished his shot. "Not from what I hear."

"Oh, now, c'mon, Unser," sighed Port, tapping his shot glass on the bar for a refill.

"C'mon nothin', that's what I heard straight from your wife's mouth, Gerry." Unser looked at Gerald.

"Essa was there?" Gerald stood up straight, stopping Port's refill mid-pour.

Unser nodded. "Well, I don't know if she was there when it happened," he added shakily, "but she was over to the vendors looking for ingredients for tonight's special, and she told me that she doubted Emmett would be the last. Th-that Timberhaven had a sickness creeping in."

"I heard it told that old Emmett was going on about… something," Port said, taking the bottle from Gerald and topping his glass off himself. "About the music's gone bad here. You know how your woman gets, though, Ger. She's young—impressionable. I dunno."

"Yeah," Gerald said, reaching under the bar for the candles. "I know just how she gets."

And Gerald lit the candles to the last window.

He was nobody's fool.

Molly

Molly looked down at the sheet of paper. It was her handwriting, she knew, but she couldn't remember writing the terrible things. They had just been on the sheet when she came out of her daze by the window.

Underneath, in the Pitch, where the hair and the vomit and the refuse of the world go, there stands a lone tower. At the top of the tower is a green, smokeless flame, a signal to Ancients who no longer see, nor do they care to, if they yet live. Acknowledgment of such a realm is unnecessary to such as they; better to forget the Pitch than to allow its existence to sully their paradigm.

But that does not serve the denizens of the Pitch.

No, it does not.

Oh yes, there be Pitchborn among that rabble, castoff from reality and forced to grow as rot does beneath a fallen branch.

The tower serves merely as a reminder to the Pitchborn that they are unwanted, and for that, they hate it. They have their hate and hunger. For all Pitchborn know hunger. It is what sustains them in the Pitch, in the Everdark. It lets them know they exist, in a reality that would rather they did not.

Molly's hands were shaking as she finished reading it a third time. She could hear Juniper seeing Jake out. She would come into the kitchen soon. Molly hid the note she didn't remember writing in the pocket of her coat and began to set the table for lunch. Somehow she had made tuna casserole. It sat, still piping hot, on top of the stove.

Another tuna casserole. What was wrong with her?

Slow

With no one seeming to be in Kings Park, Slow wandered all the way down into Old Town, stopping outside of a bar called The Pub. He sat down by a small fountain and opened his guitar.

"Here's hoping some of these locals feel generous," he thought, tuning his guitar. "I'm starving."

Slow pulled his Pignose out of his bag, hooked it to his belt, and then plugged Yvette, his guitar, into the amp. A few last-minute tweaks on the strings, and he'd be ready to start busking.

"We saw what you did." A familiar voice called out. "Sure, it took us a second to figure it out, but we saw you two in the park."

Slow looked up to see Tod, Curtis, and Bobby standing by their bikes across from him. Tod put his kickstand down and headed toward Slow. Curtis and Bobby followed.

"I'm not looking for trouble, guys," Slow told them, sliding Yvette around behind him. "She's just a little kid—a little girl."

"What do you care, black boy?" Tod demanded, "Looks to me like you made her problem your problem."

Curtis snickered and popped his knuckles while Bobby took his coat off.

Slow looked to see if anyone else was around, hoping against hope that some bystanders might see what was going on and deflate the situation. No one came.

"I'd suggest how about just me and you, one on one," Slow told Tod. "But I already know you can't fight by yourself."

"Why should I get all the fun?" Tod smiled. "Remember, guys," he said over his shoulder to Curtis and Bobby, "don't hurt the guitar. That's mine."

Then the three of them rushed Slow.

Tod went high on Slow, aiming a punch for his head, while Curtis and Bobby went low. Slow brought up his Pignose and deflected Tod's blow, but that left him open to Curtis and Bobby. They tackled Slow into the fountain, face down. Slow felt one of them punch him in the back of the head, slamming his nose into the rock fountain floor and forcing water into his throat and lungs. The clear water of the fountain turned bloody as Slow coughed, sucking down more water.

He felt himself rise out of the water as one of the guys pulled him up by Yvette, only to let him fall again as they took her from him. Slow turned over but was coughing too much to fight back when Tod sat down on his chest, forcing his head back underwater.

Slow tried to punch him, tried to resist, but he was already light-headed from all the water he'd swallowed. Everything started going dark as Tod's hands went for his throat, forcing out more air.

His last conscious thought before the world went away was that he could hear one of the guys plunking away on Yvette through the Pignose.

TWA-ANG! TWA-ANG! TWA-ANG!

And then, nothing.

Juniper

Juniper had lived with an aunt and uncle for about two months after the death of her parents. She'd hated every minute of it. They were the least imaginative people Juniper had ever known; they never read or wondered about anything, only watched television.

Juniper wasn't a huge fan of TV except for the Science channel. She occasionally enjoyed surfing the internet but mainly sought to find all her facts in books.

Molly had a lot of books and would let Juniper look through them anytime she wanted, which is one reason why Juniper enjoyed moving from her aunt and uncle's place to Molly's house.

She just wished Molly liked her better.

She didn't have time to worry about that just then, though. She needed to search Molly's collection to see if she had anything that described creatures that weren't in the encyclopedia—anything with hands for feet and lots of teeth.

She unrolled Jake's picture of the thing and looked at it again. She sat it on the floor in front of her while she looked through another bookcase, disregarding any books whose title started with *How To* or said anything about *Now A Major Motion Picture!*

She was so caught up in looking at titles that she hadn't heard Molly call her for lunch.

"What is that?" Molly's voice startled her.

Juniper looked where Molly was pointing. It was Jake's picture on the floor.

"I-it's nothing," Juniper stammered, snatching the drawing up quickly.

"Give me that drawing this instant!" Molly yelled.

Molly never yelled at Juniper, and her doing so now startled both of them. Juniper jerked the drawing around and handed it to Molly. Completely caught off-guard, Molly yelled again, "I've been calling you for lunch—get to the table!"

Juniper's eyes were wide as she stared at Molly.

Molly's hands shook again as she tried to reach out to her granddaughter, to apologize and hug the child. She hadn't meant to frighten her, but Juniper was already running for the kitchen.

Timberhaven

"Dispatch, this is Vindego, over."

"Dispatch here. What is it, Sheriff?"

"Sherry, I'm down here outside The Village. It seems we've had a performer die."

"Oh, no, Sheriff, that's awful."

"I've got Doc Waller here; he pronounced him."

"Um, Sheriff, Doc Waller's a vet."

"I know that Sherry, but Peltzer's at a physician's conference in Phoenix, and I had to call in someone."

"Yessir, Sheriff."

"Thing is, our performer, he's not a local; no identification on him. Give a call over to the JCMEO; tell them we've got one coming."

"Will do, Sheriff. Oh, and they've been calling about power being out over in the new subdivision. Kent's been working the power lines there all day, but I'm still getting calls. Now I can't reach him on his cell. If it wouldn't be a bother—"

"I'll go check on your husband once I'm done here. And Sherry? You better call in Deputy Barnhart. I know it's his day off, but…"

"*Sheriff? You there?*"

"Just call him in."

"*Yessir.*"

Sheriff Vindego hooked his radio back onto his coat and returned to disperse the crowd again as Doc Waller covered up the banjo player's lifeless form. The noon sun burned hot overhead, and still, Sheriff Vindego shivered. He'd been a sheriff in Jackson County for five years now, and while he could never explain the feeling he got while in Timberhaven, he knew not to wave it off.

Timberhaven was in for a hell of a night.

Juniper

Juniper absently poked at her bowl of tuna casserole with her fork, doing her best not to make any eye contact with Molly, who was sitting across the table from her.

"Juniper," Molly sighed. "Eat your lunch before it gets cold." She said quietly.

Juniper jumped a little at the sound of Molly's voice. The sound of Molly trying to be calm after having just yelled at her made Juniper's chin quiver, though she couldn't say why. So Molly had yelled at her, so what? Everyone these days did at some point, she thought. She forced her chin to stop quivering and ate a spoonful of tuna casserole.

After that, the two of them sat in silence, each picking at their lunch like disinterested hens pecking at seeds.

Finally, Molly broke the silence.

"I thought I'd go get the shirt for your costume tomorrow if you still need it for next weekend."

Juniper sat up straight, her eyes widened, "Did a package come for me?" she hoped.

Molly smiled. "It did. It's on the sofa in the living room."

Juniper pushed back her chair and began to hop out of it, stopping quickly and glancing at Molly with a quizzical, pleading face.

"Oh, go ahead," Molly said. "You're excused."

Juniper smiled and ran into the living room.

The package was smaller than she had hoped, with *Explosive Sparking Action!* written in letters that looked like lightning. She had read the description of her miniature Tesla coil before she'd ordered it online, but that hadn't stopped her from daydreaming that somehow the factory would mistakenly send her a *real* Tesla coil, not a sparking toy. Oh, the fun she would have had with that. She imagined Jake's reaction to such wondrously large lightning bolts, and she beamed.

It's the power of children to forget monsters, at least momentarily, in the presence of a dream come true. And as Juniper tore open the brown box, she was about to live her dream, which would make way for a new dream tomorrow. She threw packing peanuts out until she saw the inner box. It had a picture of a Tesla coil on it and Nikola Tesla's name handwritten in cursive. *Amaze your friends!* was written in neon blue and yellow with hand-drawn lightning bolts coming off of the picture.

Amaze your friends! was the part that had made her remember Jake and his monster. She still needed to do research to find out what the creature was and what it wanted. Juniper looked toward the kitchen to see if Molly was coming. She wished Molly hadn't taken Jake's drawing. She couldn't draw as well as Jake could, so she'd have to rely on her memory of what his picture looked like to do her research.

Then an idea came to her.

She grabbed the little box with the Tesla coil out of the

packing box and then put it in the pocket of her hoodie.

"Be right back!" she yelled to the kitchen.

But Molly wasn't there to hear her.

Jake

By some miracle, Jake had made it home without anyone seeing him. He slid into his room and changed out of Juniper's pants and into another pair of his own. It was a reasonably tidy room. He always made his bed and put his clothes away. Afterward, he quickly bundled Juniper's pants up into a pillowcase and hid them under his bed. He'd return them to her later when things calmed down.

Jake looked out his window to the forest behind his house. His room was the tiniest one in the house, upstairs over the garage. It wasn't a very warm room when the cold came or cool in the summer, but it let him have a great view of everything in the backyard. He often imagined wild creatures crawling up from the woods. Not like the monster that ate his pants, but bears and tigers and angry moose, and he would be able to take them all out from his bedroom window with his rifle (which was, in actuality, a long piece of PVC pipe).

And Juniper would think he was smart and brave, and she would invite him to live in her house.

Thinking about that scenario yet again, Jake almost missed seeing his brother come home with his friends. Tod carried a guitar and strummed it as they walked away from their bikes. Jake put his head up against the window so he could hear what they were saying.

"Do you think we killed him?" Bobby asked Tod.

Tod just kept strumming the guitar, with no real idea how to play it, like he was some insane rock god. "Who cares," he answered.

Curtis snickered as the three sat on the back porch.

"Do you think anyone saw us?" Bobby asked, looking around.

"What are you, on your period?" Tod asked, stopping strumming long enough to punch Bobby in the arm. Curtis snickered again. "Stop being such a little baby. Nobody saw nothin'. You think we would have been able to ride our bikes out if they had?"

Bobby didn't respond. He rubbed his arm where Tod had punched him and looked off into the forest while Tod started strumming Slow's guitar again.

Jake worried about what his brother had done. He knew that Tod liked to hit people, hurt them. But he didn't think his brother could kill someone.

"This thing sucks," Tod said, disgusted at the guitar's inability to sound good for him. He momentarily considered returning for the little speaker it had been plugged into but thought better of it. "Let's set it on fire."

Curtis smirked. "Yeah!"

Bobby smiled, too. "Where'd the barrel go that we used to burn that kid's skateboard that time?"

Tod jumped up at the suggestion, and Jake watched as the three of them disappeared around the corner with the guitar, Tod swinging it into the trash can like it was a baseball bat.

Jake didn't know why, but he felt like he had to stop his brother. He had to save that guitar. Jake ran downstairs, wondering all the way down how he could do it. His mom wasn't home, so he couldn't tell her. Jake didn't figure she would have done much to stop Tod anyhow. Ever since their dad left, she stayed at work as much as possible and let Tod do anything he wanted.

Jake thought he might call the cops without telling who he was and stop Tod that way, but his brother had beaten him badly the last time Sheriff Vindego had been by their house. Jake had been playing in the yard with no shirt on after Tod had locked him out of the house, and the sheriff had stopped by to make sure everything was okay. Once Tod assured the sheriff that Jake had gotten outside without him knowing, and the sheriff left, that's when Tod beat him up.

Jake peeked around the corner at the bottom of the stairs. It sounded to him like the three teens were in the garage, probably looking for something with which to light the fire.

Jake took the chance to look out the kitchen door to where their barrel was. There, sitting unguarded inside the metal barrel, was the guitar. It looked like Tod had strewn trash around it, hoping to use it as kindling.

Without thinking, Jake ran outside, reached into the barrel, and grabbed the guitar. It was heavier than he thought it would be, and he accidentally knocked the barrel over in his rescue of the guitar. The metal barrel gave a loud bang as it rolled down the driveway.

"What was that?" Jake heard Bobby yell from the garage.

The three teens came around from the garage just as Jake finished dragging the guitar inside the house. He stood up and locked the kitchen door.

"Jake! You little scum, open this door!" Tod yelled as he rushed up and banged on the door, staring at Jake through the window.

"Please don't hurt the guitar, Tod. It's not yours." Jake

mumbled, looking at the floor, unable to meet his brother's

angry gaze.

Tod turned to say something to Bobby and Curtis.

Curtis looked through the window at Jake and smiled, and then

both of Tod's cronies ran around the side of the house.

The front door! Jake thought, setting the guitar on the

kitchen floor and running for the living room.

"Jake!" Tod yelled, enraged.

Jake was almost at the front door.

Rodger

December 10, 1988

"I won't be gone long," Rodger put a duffle bag on the edge of the bed. Ashley, still wearing her scrubs from work even though she'd been home for hours, lay half under the covers, her eyes locked on the ceiling as Rodger talked. It had become their routine.

"I know, it's stupid," Rodger continued. He packed three days' worth of socks, boxers, t-shirts and a flannel. One pair of jeans would do him, and he didn't plan on shaving, so he zipped up the bag. "But I'm going crazy just waiting here for—"

"I'm not going to be here when you get back," Ashley spoke, not taking her eyes off the ceiling.

Hearing his wife's voice shot a warm feeling up Rodger's body, while what she said sent a shiver from the base of his skull down his back. The conflicting reactions forced Rodger to sit on the bed, collecting the duffle bag onto his lap.

"Did you hear me?" Ashley asked, finally looking at Rodger.

Rodger looked at the wedding band on his finger. It was gold, though it didn't glisten like it once did. *A decade's worth of wear will do that*, he thought. He lovingly ran his thumb over the ring. *Tarnished or not.* "I need Kiddo's unicorn for the . . . I need Uni. Is it on her bed?"

Tears slowly welled and then began to stream from Ashley's eyes as she looked back toward the ceiling.

Slow

Slow knew he wasn't okay the moment he opened his eyes. It was the music. The music had called him awake like an anxious mother late for church. The tune was noir film gray with a touch of whiskey for color; a happening bit, from what Slow had caught.

He lifted his head up off the ground, trying to remember how he'd gotten from the fountain to wherever he was.

"Am I in The Pub?" Slow thought aloud.

A natural conclusion for him to draw as Slow looked around, taking in his surroundings. There was a guy playing piano, his back to Slow. Another guy on trumpet, smooth as silk shirts. Last in the band was a young woman with skin of burnt caramel, picking a cello like a spurned lover. Once Slow locked eyes on her, he couldn't turn away.

"You gotta buy if you're gonna watch the show, House rules."

"What?" the voice broke the music's spell over Slow, and he turned to find its owner.

A small woman, at least, Slow *thought* she was a woman, was behind the bar cleaning mugs. Her head hardly came over the top of the bar.

"I said, you gotta buy if you're gonna catch the show," she repeated. "You're not gonna give me a hard time, are ya, kid?"

Slow got up from the floor and smoothed out his coat and jeans.

"Where am I?" he asked, looking around at all the empty booths and barstools that led up to the stage. "How'd I get here?"

"I won't count your 'what?' since sometimes I guess I don't make myself clear, but you only get one question for free, darlin'," the barkeep said. "So which is it gonna be?"

"Where am I?" Slow repeated.

"Cal's," was all she said as she went back to wiping mugs with her towel.

"Cal's? How'd I get here?"

"As I said, only the first one's free," she turned to replace the mug and grab a new one.

"How much does another answer cost?" Slow asked worriedly since he only had a little over three dollars to his name.

The barkeep just looked up at Slow and gave a little grin.

"That's another question," Slow said sarcastically, rolling his eyes. He reached into his pocket and counted out a dollar's worth of change. "Okay, here ya go."

The barkeep looked at the coins on her bar. "No thanks," she said, adding, "but I'd give you an answer to your second question in return for a favor."

Slow looked around the bar again.

"There's nobody else gonna help you for this cheap, darlin'," the barkeep said.

"Yeah, okay," he mumbled.

"Tell ya what I'll do," she said, putting both towel and mug down and hopping up on the bar. She stood maybe four feet tall but wasn't a little person like Slow had expected. He couldn't pinpoint just how she worked. One minute she had a child's body, then a full-grown body, yet in miniature. She kept a feminine face, but the rest of her was like cobwebs in the wind. "I'll explain Cal's, and you can just owe me that favor," she offered, her hand outstretched to Slow to seal the deal.

Slow took her hand. "Okay, I guess."

"Fantastic," she said. "Always had a soft spot for guys like you. I'm Duraine, one of the tenders here at Cal's. Calithan, the proprietor of the joint, is not presently on the grounds. He wanders a lot. Anyway, without getting too technical, Cal's provides nourishment. It tickles that part of you that quests, that creates. That being the case, a body can only get what they seek here one of four ways: sharing the words, the notes, a secret, or a favor."

Slow stared at Duraine like she'd grown a second head, but he started to follow her around the bar as she walked.

"Now, favors aren't cheap, I know, but I am giving you stellar information. More than you'd have gotten from one of the other tenders."

Slow stopped and fell to the ground as flames shot up the wall closest to them. There was no heat from it, no smoke, but it had an intense brightness that made Slow close his eyes and cover his head.

"Mind the fire," he could hear Duraine saying. "It always tries to make off with the dead."

Molly

Molly had lived in Timberhaven all of her life, which is to say she knew a thing or two about the options one had, avenues in which to figure out things that wouldn't make sense anywhere else in the world.

Once, when she was fourteen, Molly had gone away to a camp in Nebraska in an effort, as it was explained to her, to find her way. She hadn't felt lost, necessarily, certainly any more so than other kids her age, but she'd gone anyway. No fuss—just packed her bag and boarded the bus as instructed.

When she arrived at the camp, she discovered that growing up in Timberhaven had skewed her understanding of what was normal. Other kids did not, in fact, speak Fairy (which is speaking your language while thinking about what honeysuckles taste like. An easy dialect, Molly always thought.) Nor did they know or care about the connection between warts and toads (never pick up a toad who's on a quest) or that saying the phrase "graham cracker crust" really quickly and correctly at 9:03 on a Sunday night lets your Shade know where you are. (Which nobody wants to have happen at nighttime.)

In Timberhaven, these are among the many well-established facts that every Old Town Havener knows by heart before they even start grade school. Molly lived in New Town now, sure, but it didn't mean she couldn't wander her old haunts seeking guidance when the need arose. And Molly had to admit that it was long past time she figured out what was going on with her blackouts. She knew she was healthy physically—she'd just had a check-up—so that left either something was wrong with her mentally, or it was related to living in Timberhaven.

Molly wasn't prepared to deal with something being wrong with her mind, not with Juniper to look after, so her only other option was Burning Elk and his hoodoo being able to find a way to sort her out.

Molly wound around through Old Town's familiar streets and paths, down past the Fell Hotel and into the Village. She found herself enjoying the sights of handcrafted tables and colorful scarves, the smells of stout whiskeys and aged cheeses, the fires burning, and the endless chatter of haggling going on all around her.

Molly stopped at Burning Elk's tent to find nobody was home. There was just a sign hanging from a wire that read *Gone*. Molly looked around when she heard someone calling her name.

"He is not here, Molly," a voice came from the tent next door. "He is gone down to the river to speak to it about his brother."

"Oh, okay, Pela," Molly said, ignoring the confusing element of the statement. Instead, she asked, "Did he say how long he might be?"

Pela had looked to be a woman in her mid-forties ever since Molly, who herself was in her late fifties, was a little girl.

Whatever gypsy magic that kept Pela young seemingly did not affect her disposition toward Molly, though, as Pela had disapproved of her ever since a reasonably innocent indiscretion with Burning Elk in Molly's teenage years took place.

"No," Pela said, absently fingering a purple scarf from a collection at the tent next door, "he did not. What is it we can do for you?"

"I," Molly began, not sure how to explain anything. "No, I'll just come back by later."

Pela looked up from the scarves, "You are having troubles. Troubles you wonder if my *staruszek* can assist you with," Pela started picking over a table of jewelry. "He cannot."

Pela only threw Polish at Molly when she was in a particularly nasty mood, and Molly was no longer interested in listening to her. She had come for help from Burning Elk, not to be lorded over by his petulant wife, partner, whatever Pela was to him. But then Molly noticed that the more annoyed she got with Pela, the more Molly felt like a fog was lifting. She began thinking more clearly, more like herself.

The quickness of it forced her to sit down on the ground.

"Are you okay?" A man walking by asked.

"I really don't know," Molly replied.

Juniper

Tearing through a field, Juniper rounded the corner of a beat-up '69 Buick Skylark at a run. She had kept the pace all the way from her house, stopping only occasionally to check and see if she saw Jake's monster anywhere. She hadn't.

Her hope was that Story could shed some light on things, traveled as she was, and practiced in the way of monster-seeing. Juniper only slowed down once she'd arrived at the junkyard and opened the door to her laboratory.

"Story?" she asked the room, "I know you need a catnap, but I wondered if I could ask you about a monster really quick."

Story slept in her usual spot, high near the rafters, in an old picnic basket that didn't have a top. She peeked up over the lip and yawned.

"I'm here, Juniper," the cat replied sleepily. "What can I help you with?"

"Well, just really quick, can I ask about Jake's monster?" Juniper pled, continuing without waiting for Story to answer. "See, Jake was at my house but then had to leave. Only he said that he saw a monster on his way home who tried to eat him but only got his pants, and we were wondering—"

Something got Story's attention, forcing the cat to sit bolt upright in the basket, her eyes wide.

"Juniper!" she yelled, hopping down from the basket and heading over to a beat-up old school backpack. "We've got to go now!"

Whenever Juniper and Story left the junkyard together, Story always rode in the backpack. She was almost always traveling, so Juniper didn't mind playing a taxi. Cats get tired and need a break from the road from time to time, Juniper figured.

She picked up the backpack and put it on with Story inside. She struggled a little bit, pulling it over her bulky hoodie.

"What's the matter?" Juniper asked as they left the laboratory.

"We've got to hurry to Jake's house!" the cat said from the depths of the backpack.

Juniper started to run. "Is he okay?" she worried.

"Just hurry!" was all Story replied.

Juniper ran faster.

Jake

Jake nearly hadn't locked the front door in time, turning the deadbolt just as Curtis and Bobby reached the handle. Then, he ran back to the kitchen as Tod began kicking the back door.

"You are dead!" Tod yelled between kicks.

Jake grabbed the guitar and began dragging it upstairs as quickly as he could manage. He figured he could hide it someplace before Tod got in the house. The guitar thumped on the stairs, almost in tune with the thumps from Tod, Curtis, and Bobby, trying to get back inside.

"I've just got to…make it up two more stairs." Jake counted.

He heard glass break from downstairs, but he couldn't be sure if it had come from the living room or the kitchen. Either way, the other boys would be inside soon. Jake's heart beat hard. He'd never done anything to make Tod as angry as he was then. He hoped his brother didn't kill him.

Jake finished hiding the guitar and ran back out into the hall just as footsteps came thundering up the stairs. He dove into the bathroom and shut the door, locking it. Then he ran to the window and desperately tried to pull it up, praying to Santa that he could get it open just enough to climb out.

It rose, but not enough. Jake pulled again, edging it up a little further.

Somebody hit the bathroom door.

"Open up!" Tod yelled.

"Please don't, Tod!" Jake yelled back to the splintering door.

"The little stain's in here," Tod told one of the other boys in the hall.

"Does he have the guitar?" Bobby asked.

"Dunno," Tod said. "Trash his room and look for it. He's always hiding stupid crap all over in there. I'll take care of him."

Jake whimpered, trying his best not to cry. He realized as tears slid down his face that he wasn't going to be able to fit out the bathroom window before Tod broke through the door.

His brother kicked the door again, splintering it at the hinges.

Jake's heart raced.

Slow

Slow dove back from the fire-strewn wall, crawling backward until he was up against a chair, as Duraine giggled.

"That's enough, D," the cello player announced from the stage.

Duraine's lips pursed as she glowered back in response.

"Boy's got a right to get the ins and outs of Cal's without you tormenting him," the woman continued.

"Mind your own business, Twist," Duraine spat.

"Am I dead?" Slow asked the room.

Duraine laughed hard, choking. Twist came over to Slow and offered him a hand up.

"Let's get you upright, eh, kiddo?" Twist said, smiling the kind of smile that department store clerks offer small, lost children.

Slow got to his feet and looked back to the wall that had been coated in flames seconds ago, only to find it had returned to being a plain, simple wall. In disbelief, Slow walked over

116

and touched it, his fingers shaking. He looked back at Duraine and Twist.

"What is happening?" he asked, his lower lip quivering.

"Put this one on my tab," Twist told Duraine, who lost her smile in the telling. "Look, kid, sit down for a second, and I'll try and explain some things. But you've got to stop just throwing out questions like that," Twist gestured to a table nearby and pulled a chair out for herself. "Guys," she looked to her partners on the stage, "let's take five."

The pianist shrugged and got up, stretching. The trumpet player nodded but kept playing, using his mute to serenade the room with a lonely blues melody.

Slow took the chair opposite Twist and watched Duraine slink back to the bar; her mood completely changed from mischievous to dark.

"You've got to watch the tenders here," Twist began, "they're not all that they seem. You got lucky; Duraine's not so bad. There are others that wouldn't have given you up so easily."

"What's a—" Slow caught himself. "Sorry," Not asking questions was difficult when up is not and left meant fuzzy.

Twist smiled again. "It's okay. A tender is a—it is something that keeps the bar safe while Calithan's away walking."

Slow nodded his head as Twist spoke. He recognized almost every word she had spoken, but they hadn't made sense in the order she'd said them. So nodding seemed appropriate.

"This is his bar, Calithan's," Twist extended her arm, pointing around the room. "He's done a lot in keeping the Songs safe."

As a bluesman, Slow desperately wanted to ask more about which songs, but he was a quick study—at least he was when walls didn't erupt in flames for no reason and throw him off his game—so he kept his questions to himself. But Twist seemed to read him too well.

"It's quiet tonight, I know. Just me and my boys here. But I've got one helluva tab, so I take any open shift," Twist said. "Even the dead ones. Some of the other shifts, you'd have a hard go of getting a table. It levels out when Cal's not in. All the big talent shows up when he's here. Wanna show him something he's never seen before," she scoffed. "Like that ever happens. Calithan knows Songs from before Time. Before night and day was a thing. Even knows a few that never came to be."

"So this is his place," Twist explained, snapping Slow out of his daydream about songs that never were. "And you must have gone down someplace too near the Gate, got sucked in before proper opening time."

"So I'm not dead," Slow said, matter-of-factly to avoid it sounding like a question.

"Not yet," Twist said, leaving Slow not overly reassured. "But something's wrong on your side; else, you would have slid back when the fire scared you."

"Is there—" Slow gritted his teeth. "I sometimes wonder if there is any way out of this bar," Slow started, thinking as he spoke, "since I don't see any doors or any windows that a guy could slide through, but then I remember that I can't ask questions without paying an arm and a leg. Possibly literally."

Twist laughed right out loud. "Clever, kid," her look changed and became more serious. "But you're right; there's no way out of Cal's Bar short of sliding."

"Show's what you know," Duraine muttered, eavesdropping from the bar.

Twist and Slow turned to her.

"Clearly, you have something you want to share," Twist said. "But I have no intention of adding any more questions to my tab, and the kid already owes you a favor."

"He could still pay in words, notes, or secrets," Duraine said, a smile splitting her face.

<u>Rodger</u>

December 11, 1988

Rodger pulled the car to a stop in front of an older-style house. Though covered in snow, Rodger could tell it was well-maintained. Someone had cleared the walkway leading up to the front door, and he could see a lit Christmas tree through the bay window.

Rodger had driven through the night, only sliding three times on the roads during the trip, which he thought was solid car handling on his part, given the time of year. He checked his reflection in the rearview mirror and tsked the bags under his eyes, the shadows on his face.

"I look like a zombie," he said to the empty back seat. His throat tightened, but he shook it off and looked back to the Christmas tree before opening his car door and going toward what he hoped might offer some guidance.

Molly

Pela wandered on, picking her way through the Village, and left Molly alone, sitting in the dirt. The fog started to seep back into and over Molly's mind again, causing her to tear up. This time, though, they were tears of anger. She didn't like feeling so helpless. Molly wanted to fight whatever was causing her to be less than she was, but she didn't know how to fight it—*who* to fight.

Molly got up and dusted herself off as people shuffled around her. She could look for Burning Elk at the river, of course, but she couldn't be sure that she wouldn't black out in the middle of the woods on the way down, and that wasn't a risk she was willing to take yet. The woods in Timberhaven, while awe-inspiring most of the time, could occasionally make anyone who isn't mindful different.

Altered.

And Molly'd had it with being altered. She needed answers from someone. Someone to help her figure things out so she could take care of Juniper.

Juniper.

Thinking about her made Molly equally happy and sad. She loved the child, wished fervently that she could get Juniper to like her back—if not love her—so that they could be a family. They were all that was left. She felt like they were two corks stuck in a draining sink. Forced together as the world spins in unfair and mean, but going under at different intervals.

Molly started walking. She didn't know where she was headed, but she was aware of walking, which was something. At least she wasn't dazed—blacked out. Molly was merely ignorant, wandering the path of the inspired.

She tried to remember everything that she'd ever heard Burning Elk teach. The man was always teach-talking, which Molly sometimes took in as white noise. It's not that she hadn't paid attention, she had, but Burning Elk would happily switch from saying he'd like ham and eggs for breakfast to catching

the blue edges of the world and describing what it was that he

peeked mid-breakfast order.

Blue was important, Molly knew. Blue was where the

secrets kept, wrapped up in a song of making. She could never

See as Burning Elk could, but Molly could always sing.

She just needed to know which song could get her out

of this mess.

Singers make the peace they need—the healing of

simple things like bad moods or Mondays—by humming a

melody, and they do so without even having to think about it.

Molly's problem would mean seeking out which song. She

feared it might not be any of the songs she knew already.

Wouldn't she have sung it by this time if that had been the

case? Though, who knew, with the way her brain was acting

lately.

Molly continued walking, determined, if without a plan.

She crossed through a crowd listening to a man dressed only in trash bags reciting the Magna Carta from memory, and she was more than a little surprised that he *had* a crowd.

Up the old rock stairs (carved by stonemasons said to have come to Timberhaven after they had finished up in Stonehenge) and across the Valley of the Dolls (a symposium of mannequins dressed in varying styles that changed by the day, at the time they were the League of Nations) into the property surrounding the Fell Hotel.

The grass was perfectly manicured around the hotel, with flower beds angled to make a small maze that one could navigate. A birdbath of Beowulf fighting Grendel was at its center. Molly walked around it, taking the quickest path to the hotel's side door through the kitchen.

"What 'ave we 'ere?" a man stirring a smoking pot asked her. He wore a floral-patterned apron that read *Let Me Chop Your Suey* and a Bedazzled chef's hat, gifts from his niece in Atlanta, who seemed to think he wasn't colorful enough.

Molly waved him off, "I don't have time today, Hector. And your French accent needs work."

"What do you meen?" Hector scoffed, "I am ze French!"

Molly just kept walking, determined. She left the kitchen and headed for the main lobby, still not sure what she was walking toward, only following where she was being pulled.

"Molly?"

She turned to look up the staircase at whoever had called her name.

And fainted.

Juniper

Juniper watched the Steadherd house from the forest. She could make out through the bedroom window that Tod, Curtis, and Bobby were tearing Jake's room apart.

"Story, what do we do?" she asked worriedly. "You don't think that Jake…" she let the question dangle.

"He's fine, for now," Story told her from the backpack. "I'm not quite rested enough from my journey to See how I'd like to, but I can tell you that Jake isn't in his bedroom."

Juniper shivered as she watched the house, her eyes darting to other windows in the hope that Jake might be there. She started wishing she had encouraged him more while he was drawing the monster.

"What is it about these boys?" Story asked, noticing Juniper's fear. "I wish you would tell me."

Story knew things about people. Where they had been, where they were, and where they were going. Juniper had found it amazing when Story told her about the ability. She'd wondered if all cats could do it.

"Not all," Story had told her, explaining as best she could, "but nor am I the only cat who can."

Story had said she would never read Juniper's secrets, though, out of their being friends and all. Juniper hadn't seen what the big deal was, but now she was glad that Story didn't know.

"They're just mean, is all," Juniper said by way of explanation, "and I worry for Jake."

Juniper could feel Story giving a tut-tut look from inside the backpack.

"Fine, keep your secrets," the cat said quietly, adding, "it seems you aren't the only one with them. Stay still! The boys are leaving."

Juniper dove down on her belly, trying her best to shrink down into the bed of the forest. The back door of the house slammed open as Tod and his crew came outside, Tod screaming in frustration.

"The bathroom window was open. He must've gotten out with it." Bobby said.

Tod punched him so quickly that, at first, Juniper didn't know what had happened.

"I know that!" Tod yelled. "I don't know how he did it, but the little turd escaped."

Curtis snickered, staring down at Bobby on the ground.

"Shut up," Tod turned on Curtis. "Or I'll hit you, too."

Curtis stopped. Bobby got up off the ground and wiped his hand across his freshly bloodied nose.

"Let's ride, see if we find him," Tod said, picking up his bike. "He can't have got far with that guitar."

The three boys gathered up their bikes and rode away. Juniper still waited another ten minutes before she got up. She looked back at the house.

"What should we do?" Juniper asked.

"Let's go inside. They won't be back for a while," the cat replied.

Juniper picked up her backpack and slowly, ever so slowly, crept toward the house and the still slightly open back door.

Rodger

December 11, 1988

"This is her favorite toy?" a tall, plump woman in a cream-colored housedress asked Rodger, taking a stuffed unicorn with blue, glass eyes and pink yarn for hair from him.

"Yes, Uni," Rodger said, his hands aching to follow the toy to keep it a moment longer. "She's a—we watched the *Dungeons and Dragons* cartoon together when it was on. She's always loved unicorns, and how Uni talks makes her laugh."

The woman went to a small kitchen table and placed the toy there but continued to the oven. She picked up and motioned a tea kettle to Rodger.

"No, thank you," Rodger shook his head. He was still standing in the doorway to the kitchen. He didn't know that he believed in psychics in any regard, but this was certainly not how he'd envisioned things starting.

"Please, sit," the woman said, gesturing to the table. Rodger took the seat across from where she'd sat Uni. He first put his hands in his lap, then moved them to the table. Palms up, then palms down, thinking the woman might mistake the action as his mocking her.

"Sorry," Rodger explained. " I, ahem, this is my first time talking to someone with your…abilities." He placed his hands back in his lap.

"It's okay," the woman smiled, coming over to the table with a cup of hot water and a tea bag. She sat down and began to bounce the bag into the cup, though not looking as she did so. She stayed focused on the stuffed unicorn. "My name is Elaina, Mr. Foster, and I think I can help you."

Jake

Jake didn't move.

He hadn't heard anything in the house for almost twenty minutes, but still, he did not make a peep. His legs had cramped terribly, bent up like he was, hiding inside the wicker clothes hamper. He listened as hard as he could.

No sound.

Suddenly, he could hear movement downstairs. Jake held his breath.

"Jake?" Juniper whispered.

"Juniper?" he answered as he poked his head up from under the hamper lid. The dirty clothes he'd hidden under fell to the floor.

"Where are you?" Juniper asked more loudly.

"I'm in the bathroom," Jake said. "Come help me out of here; my legs got pins and needles!"

Juniper came in and helped Jake climb out of the hamper.

"Are you okay?" she asked.

"I think so," Jake said, rubbing his legs. Juniper was looking at the busted bathroom door. "Jeez, Tod was really after me."

"What for this time?" Juniper asked, picking up a big splinter from the door.

"Wait, I'll show ya," Jake said, walking out into the hall. Juniper followed.

The two made their way down the hall to Tod's door. He usually locked it, but it was open a crack as they got to it. Jake pushed the door open and walked in, climbing under Tod's bed.

"Jake, come on," Juniper said. "Let's get out of here." Being in Tod's room frightened her. It terrified Jake, too.

"Hold on, I gotta get it," he said, his legs dangling from under Tod's bed.

"What is it?" Juniper asked.

"They were gonna burn it, but I saved it," came Jake's muffled explanation as he heaved something across the floor. "I put it in his room instead of mine and then hid in the hamper."

"Very clever!" Story said from the backpack.

Jake came from under the bed and pulled a guitar free behind him. Juniper gasped at the sight of it.

"It's Slow's," she whispered.

"Yeah," Jake said. "I think Tod and the others did something to him."

Juniper ran her fingers over the guitar and the scuff marks where Tod had hit things with it. It had a broken string, too, but otherwise, it looked okay to her. She took it from Jake.

"It's heavy," she said.

"Bring the guitar and let's get out of here," Story said quietly from the backpack.

"If Slow's hurt, though, Story, can we find him?" Juniper asked as she took the guitar and made her way back downstairs. Jake shut Tod's door behind them.

"He's in a place, well, it's not anywhere I would be willing to take you, Juniper. It's far too dangerous," Story said from the backpack. "Maybe, once he's left there."

The trio left Jake's house by the back door.

"Wait," Jake yelled and ran back inside.

"Jake, come on!" Juniper whispered back.

"I'll be quick," Jake yelled down the stairs.

"It's okay, Juniper," Story said.

Juniper paced the back porch back and forth with nervous energy. Something dawned on her.

"Hey, you talked in front of Jake," she said, turning to look over her shoulder at the backpack. "You've never done that before."

"It's no matter," Story replied.

"But," Juniper thought aloud, "he didn't seem to hear you."

"As it should be," Story said.

Jake came running downstairs with Juniper's pants.

"Here ya go. Thanks!"

With a sigh, Juniper led them back into the forest. It wasn't long before the guitar got too heavy for Juniper to carry on her own, weaving in and out of trees and up and down hills, so she took one end and let Jake take the other.

"So what *can* we do?" Juniper asked, looking over her shoulder to make sure no one was following them.

"I dunno," Jake answered. "Maybe lunch?"

"I meant about Slow," Juniper told him, but softened a bit, saying, "I've got some figs in the backpack with Story if you're hungry."

Jake's eyes went wide, matching his smile.

"Really?" he said, reaching up into her backpack and nearly dropping his end of the guitar.

"Jake!" Juniper yelled.

Story shushed them. "We've got to be quiet," she explained. "I know where Jake's brother and his friends are, but if there are other things out in these woods tonight, I'm not rested enough yet to be of much help if they find you."

"We need a plan," Juniper said, setting the guitar down long enough to get Jake a fig. "How do we help Slow?"

"I've got an idea of where to start," Story said, trying to meow supportively from inside her makeshift taxi, "but you're not going to like it, Juniper."

"Where?" Juniper asked suspiciously.

"We need to go see Willoughby." Story said.

"Willoughby?" Juniper scoffed.

Jake, having grown accustomed to Juniper's talking to herself and who was happily munching on his fig, smiled a broad smile that twinkled his eyes at the mention of Willoughby. Juniper only moaned and rolled her eyes.

Slow

What's a Niksik? Slow wondered to himself, having never been more confused in his life. He wanted to ask so many questions but knew better than to ask in that room. Wherever that room was.

"The Niksik are not an option for him; he'd never survive," Twist explained as she got up from the table and headed to the bar. "And since when are you helpful?"

Duraine pouted. "I'm helpful. Didn't I, just last week, help that tiger fella find his game?"

"Sure, after you took it and twisted the rules," Twist said. "She never helps unless there's something in it for her," she told Slow.

"Nothing either of you says makes any sense," Slow stood from his chair at the table. "I want to go back to…my familiar world. I want to leave here." He walked over to the small stage. "I thought I wanted to play The Pub. I'd heard that every great bluesman ever at some point played a gig at a dive bar in Timberhaven."

"Hey, now!" Duraine hollered from the bar. Twist stopped her from chucking a mug at Slow.

"But it's this bar, not that one, and I can't make sense of things here," Slow continued, "I don't understand anything, and I think maybe I *am* dead." Slow remembered the pain in the fountain outside of The Pub, the feeling of Tod's fists.

"You're not dead," Twist sighed, looking down at the bar, "not yet. Your song is still playing on the other side, which means you're still in it. It's touch and go, though, so you've got to hurry and get back."

"Why are you so interested in helping this one?" Duraine asked, her face twisted with suspicion.

Slow found that he was interested in the answer too.

Twist sighed. "We need to think of something else besides the Niksik. Here," Twist grabbed a paper menu from the bar and brought it back to the table. "Let's try this."

Duraine snorted. "Ha! You, using magic," she came over to the table, her towel still in her hand. "This I gotta see."

Slow met them back at the table. "I'll do whatever I need to." He'd had to rethink his phrasing so it didn't come out as a question.

"Shut up, D," Twist looked at the small woman in annoyance. "Okay, kid, here's what's gonna go down. I want you to take this menu, and I want you to write on it with this," she dug lipstick out of her pocket. It was dark green and had pocket fuzz on it. "On one side, write where you are and where you wanna be on the other."

Slow took the lipstick and looked at the menu. It was sideways, but he could still make out the words *slow burn* and *casualty of funk*, both having *memory of a birthday* written in under Cost.

"He's just looking at it, Twist," Duraine said absently. "Maybe he doesn't know how to, to whatcha call it, write."

"I can write just fine," Slow said, turning the lipstick so he could write more easily. He wrote *Cal's Bar* on one side and *The Pub* on the other. When he finished, Twist took it from him and folded the menu in half so that both of the things he wrote would be touching. Slow closed his eyes, though he couldn't say what he was expecting to happen.

"Hmmm," Twist took the menu and went over to where a candle was burning at another table. She held the menu over the flame and chanted some words that Slow had never heard before. Duraine scoffed and headed back to the bar.

"You two, you're cute, with your," she lowered her voice, mimicking Slow, "'I don't know how I got here,' and your," she pointed at Twist and did a falsetto voice, "'I'm gonna use magic.' I could just eat you up. I won't, but I could."

Twist stared at the folded-up menu, turning it over and over like a kid trying to figure out a magic trick. "That should have worked," she muttered.

Slow stood and listened to the trumpeter wind down his song. It sounded familiar.

"You listening to me, kid?" Twist asked.

"Sorry," Slow stammered. "I was listening to—sorry."

"I said the lunch crowd will be coming in soon, and you don't want to be around here then," Twist pulled him by the arm back up to the bar. "I hate this plan, but Duraine's idea is the only one that gets you out of here in time."

"He's got to drink first, Twist," Duraine said, holding up a shot glass with something black and angry inside. "And you *can't* put this on *your* tab."

No stranger to alcohol, Slow grabbed the shot. "No problem."

Twist caught him by the wrist. "Fool boy, you don't even know what it is you're doing. Now, when you're there, don't take anything you get offered."

"Don't offer anything you don't want to be taken, either," Duraine interrupted.

Twist looked at her. "You're helping now?"

"I thought we were doing a buddy bit," Duraine huffed. "What, diva, you prefer to work alone?"

"Fine," Twist rolled her eyes. "Slow, most importantly, before you drink this, you've got to follow *your* song to make it through the Niksik. If you lose track of it, let it change into some other tune…"

"You'll be one of the Niksik," Duraine finished.

Slow thought about that for a long time—*his* song. He knew the song that they meant.

"I'm ready." And he took the shot.

<u>Molly</u>

When Molly came to, she was lying in a big feather bed, and a maid wearing an apron that had *Fell Hotel* written on it was setting down a tray of tea and little sandwiches.

"What happened?" Molly asked, sitting up.

"Sorry, ma'am, but you collapsed," The maid replied, straightening the tray on the end table.

"Oh," Molly vaguely remembered. "Where's Jacobi—er, I mean, Mr. Fell?"

"He'll be along presently, I should think, ma'am. I'll leave you to it." The maid gave a small curtsy and left the room.

Molly looked at the tray and realized that she was ravenously hungry. She grabbed two of the little sandwiches, downed one of them, and reached for the tea to wash it down. She'd be the first to admit she wasn't overly fond of cucumbers, but the sandwiches hit the spot.

"That's what I like to see," Jacobi said from the doorway. "You need to get your strength back up."

Jacobi Fell had a silver tongue that matched his silver hair. He and Molly had known each other for years, long before either had met their prospective spouses, and while there may have been a time when each had wondered "what if" about the other, Fate had cast them as friends first, and firmly.

"Jacobi, sorry about this."

Jacobi tutted away her apology. "What's a little fainting among friends?" His look turned serious. "Molly, what's going on? I've sent Audrey after Burning Elk. You were muttering his name after you passed out."

Molly drank deeply from her mug of tea. "It's—I'm not sure how to explain it, Jacobi. I've been…"

"Off," Jacobi finished her thought. "I've seen it before, you know," he put his hands on either side of Molly's face and looked into her eyes, examining. "But never in you."

Molly pulled away slowly. "It's not—I mean, I've been losing time—blacking out. I keep finding strange things written in my handwriting that I don't recall ever writing. Horrible things, Jacobi, about creatures and filth."

"Slow down," Jacobi said as he refilled her mug with hot tea from the pot and handed it back to her. "Audrey will be back soon with Burning Elk. We'll get things sorted."

"What if the problem's not Timberhaven but with me?" Molly wondered for the hundredth time. "I've got a little one to look after."

"Ah, yes, your granddaughter!" Jacobi's face, and thereby the room, came to life. "I've yet to meet her. Juniper, yes?"

"Yes," Molly flushed, the abrupt change of subject startled her, but she embraced it. "She's a young lady's just turned eight not more than a month ago," Molly beamed. "Smart as a whip, too."

"A scientist, if I'm not mistaken," Jacobi said as he walked over to the closet.

"Right again," Molly said. "But how did you—"

"Audrey, as you know, hears everything," Jacobi said, pulling a wrapped package out from the closet. It was orange with a green bow and a tag with Juniper's name. "Apologize for its lateness, won't you?"

Rodger

December 11, 1988

"I sense her," Elaina whispered. Her eyes were rolling back into her head as she clutched Melinda's toy. "She's in a black forest. There's a stream someplace nearby—no, not a stream. Maybe waves? The sea?"

Rodger stayed quiet for a beat. Two. Until he finally muttered, "We live in middle America, ma'am. Nowhere near an ocean."

"Still, that's what I hear," Elaina said. Her head cocked to the side, listening. "A breeze is blowing off the hidden sea, dancing throughout the forest cloaked in midnight. Your little girl is…there's something—"

Rodger jumped back in his chair, nearly tripping out of it as Elaina's head slammed once into the table. When she uprighted once again, her eyes had gone white.

"ThEre are mONsteRS here, dADdy," Melinda's disembodied voice was coming from the psychic's mouth. "TeETh in thEIR hANds and eyEBallS in their MouTHS."

Juniper

Juniper and Jake had hidden Slow's guitar near a giant rock that they had found together at the beginning of the summer, burying it under sticks and leaves the best they could. Dirt, Juniper thought, might damage the guitar.

Then, to Jake's delight, they were headed back out of the forest.

"There's still a monster, you know," he'd kept mentioning as they walked.

The edge of The Fell Hotel's property, and thereby the northern edge of Old Town, was contained in a high, red stone wall standing eight feet tall. Above it, iron bars with spear tips at the end of each. Juniper and Jake walked along the base of the wall, running their hands along the artwork graffiti that was painted all over it. Bridges and buildings were drawn there from all around the world and other worlds, too. An ugly troll fought a gallant knight under a banner of silver oak here while a rocket rounded a red moon there.

Juniper loved examining the intricate details hidden all over the wall. Or would have, had Willoughby not lived there.

Jake's eyes filled with joy as he searched the wall over, scouring the artwork for a sign of the first and only real bit of Timberhaven's magic that he had ever seen.

Willoughby was a chalk drawing who typically stood no more than two inches tall, though he could grow and shrink as he liked, of a little man wearing a purple shirt with a dragon on it, a California highway patrolman's helmet, big sunglasses circa the 1970s, and enormous, gray swimming flippers. He also happened to talk and moved endlessly around the collage, so one never knew where to find him.

Juniper stopped and looked around to make sure no one could see them. She sighed and then looked up at the drawings, trying to catch some movement.

"Willoughby," she whispered. "Willoughby, come out here; it's important."

Jake looked back and forth at the wall, smiling.

"Willoughby," Juniper said a little louder.

"Say, *Sir* Willoughby," a tinny little voice said from somewhere on the mural, but Juniper couldn't pinpoint it. Jake giggled.

"Hush, Jake," Juniper said. She squinted a double-take at a clockwork Labrador's eye but hadn't, it turned out, seen Willoughby there. "Willoughby, we need help."

"You know the rules," Willoughby's voice came again.

"Enough, Willoughby," Story said with a slight meow of reproach. "We haven't the time."

Suddenly the faceplate of the knight fighting the troll came up. "Sorry, Story," Willoughby said, his voice no longer tinny. He popped from the knight's armor onto a mermaid from a merry-go-round painted under a starry sky. "Didn't see you there," he continued, giving the mermaid a futile giddy-up. "Happy to be of service."

"Neat!" Jake exclaimed.

"Jake!" Juniper shushed him. "Willoughby, we need to ask you something, and we'd like a straight answer."

"I've only crooked answers, but there's a hammer over there," Willoughby pointed to a Viking warrior landing a crushing blow with a war hammer onto an unfortunate demon's head, "that you could probably straighten them out with."

Juniper sighed. Willoughby was always difficult, but he was way worse when it came to her, Juniper thought.

"Willoughby," Story said.

"Apologies, but I don't get many visitors these days, and I do like to talk," Willoughby smiled, having teleported to a race car at eye level with Juniper. "Ask away, Doctor Soot," Willoughby often playfully mocked Juniper's love of science.

Jake laughed and tried to touch Willoughby's face peeking out of the race car, but Willoughby had already popped back up and was perusing something that a man in a 1950s-style office building was typing out.

"Jake, stop," Juniper said. "You're as bad as he is," she looked back up to Willoughby. "We are looking for our friend and wondering about a monster that may have come into New Town."

"Alas," Willoughby said. "I can answer but one question per customer."

Juniper thought for a moment. "Okay, where's Slow."

Willoughby stammered, thrown off by Juniper's quick decision, but then sat on a drawing of Rodin's The Thinker, mimicking the pose.

"Your friend…I'm sorry," Willoughby appeared in front of Juniper's face again. This time he removed his helmet. "But your friend is in two places at one time."

Juniper's face went ashen. "Is, is he dead?"

"That is not for me to say," Willoughby bowed. "But rarely, if ever, is it a good thing to be in two places at once," he thought again, adding, "You need to go see the giant killer, in the name, if not action, for what to do next."

"I don't know what that means!" Juniper yelled.

"Juniper, calm down," Story said from the backpack. "Thank you, Willoughby. Juniper, we'll figure it out. Make your payment."

Juniper picked up a stick of charcoal from the many scattered around the ground in front of the wall. She drew in, poorly, a pair of black socks on the mural, with the left one having a hole in it.

Willoughby harrumphed but still inspected the socks with a smile.

"Okay," Juniper added. "Your turn, Jake."

Jake smiled and then yelled. "WHAT'S THE MONSTER THAT ATE MY PANTS?"

"Wait, what?" Willoughby said, thinking their business concluded, he felt quite bewildered.

"You said one question a customer. Jake's up next," Juniper smiled.

Willoughby admitted his defeat with a sigh. "Fine, fine," he scrunched up his face. Then, if drawings could go pale, Juniper was sure Willoughby was doing so. "The creature is not of this world. It's not—it won't be sated with a small taste like before, no. It has been trapped these many years, using your monster—one of its kin—as an antenna, stuck here as a signal. In between—in a hole with a view—to get to nibble but never bite. It hungers. It hungers so much."

Juniper shivered. The thought of the thing from Jake's picture being real scared her.

Jake had been drawing a baseball and glove on the wall while Willoughby explained things and finished up his drawing with a master's focus. He already knew that the monster that had eaten his pants was real, after all, and so could get no more scared of it than he already was.

Slow

Slow was walking before he was fully awake. He felt the wind on his face and somehow knew that he was walking alongside a cliff, maybe at the edge of an ocean? He couldn't be sure. He could hear and feel the crunch of frosted grass underfoot, but it was as though he was walking on a moonless night out in the country. No ambient light to guide his way; just going by feel alone.

It wasn't like waking up in Cal's Bar; this time, he knew *how* he'd arrived.

He just didn't know where he was.

The maybe ocean slammed into the side of the cliff and made him feel as though he should walk further from its edge. Or at least where he imagined the cliff's edge to be.

Not knowing where he was, again, made Slow feel frustrated. He'd grown tired of being out of control of where he went, where he was going. His focus slipped from his frustration onto the low rumble of the crashing waves.

Slow stopped walking for a minute and looked toward the sound of their crashing.

In the sound, beneath it, he could hear more. The rumbling was carried by screams of pain, like chanting monks in eternal agony. It crashed, a crescendo of raw nerves and angry energy, only to roll back again in a furious nightmare of matter, all of it out in darkness beyond shadow.

Beyond Slow.

Beyond, but around him and in him, still. He could follow the sound, the notes, picking and choosing which beats were him and which were not in a symphony of was/now/ maybe that left him breathless. Beauty in chaos. The self exposed as a lie. Individuality as a cautionary tale. Better to be counted as We rather than I.

Safety in numbers.

Slow was all but lulled in, sensing warmth in what he could not see in a masterpiece of tonality.

But for one section.

A riff.

It didn't fit the piece at all, but it was unmistakably there. Slow heard it.

And in hearing it, Slow remembered it.

His riff.

A piece that he wrote after playing with Cincinnati; she, a Delta Blue, Nina Simone dream— the best night of his life. The strongest notion of romantic love that Slow had yet to feel at his young age. It was light, and it was life. A happy jazz tune born of a bluesman for a Queen.

Slow heard it. His fingers, aching for Yvette's strings, played it on the open air.

The waves crashed louder, harder.

But it was too late.

Slow heard *his* song.

He walked on.

Molly

Molly took the gift from Jacobi.

"Thank you, but you didn't need to."

"Nonsense," Jacobi said, offering Molly's refilled cup of tea back to her. "It's nothing. A telescope that we found lying around. I hope she likes it."

"She'll love it," Molly said. Talking about Juniper had helped her focus again. "Jacobi," Molly said softly, "I need to —what I mean is, I must ask a favor of you."

"Anything that's within my power is yours," Jacobi said, sitting in a chair across from the bed. "You should know that."

Molly took a breath. "If whatever is going on with me —whether it's my mind or…something else, I need to know that Juniper will be okay. That she'll be looked after and not left to the means of the State."

"Now, Molly, I'm sure it won't come to that," Jacobi said, smiling. "You're a vibrant woman! You'll come out of this fine. You'll see."

"Just the same," Molly pushed. "I need to hear you say the words. If I don't make it, if I can't take care of my granddaughter, you'll see to it," Molly quickly added, "there's nobody else I can ask."

Jacobi's splendor diminished a little bit, and he looked at his feet like a little boy.

"Of course, Molly. Of course."

With the matter settled, Molly hopped out of bed reenergized. "Granted, that's not the ending to this tale that we're hoping for," she headed across the room to where her shoes were on the floor. "Now, a game plan. That's what we need. A plan of attack. As to what I'll be attacking, I don't know yet, but that's merely what lesser people would consider a problem."

"Do tell," Jacobi smiled. "Don't stop now; you're on a roll."

There was a knock at the door.

"Come in!" Molly said a little too loudly.

"I, uh, sorry," a girl with bright blue hair peeked her head into the room. "I've got Burning Elk with me."

"Audrey, I'm sorry, come in, come in," Molly said, hugging the teenage girl once she was inside. "Your hotel here is amazing; it seems I'm bursting with enthusiasm."

Behind Audrey came a tall, lean man who looked to be in his early forties at the oldest. Molly knew better.

"Burning Elk, thank you for coming," Molly said, hugging the man.

With the hug broken, Burning Elk looked into Molly's eyes and grinned.

"There's the girl I know," he said. "Seems you've got a touch of the pixie about you. I can see it there, in your hair."

Molly played with a piece of her hair and looked at Jacobi. "The tea?"

"You needed something to clear the cobwebs," Jacobi said, clearing his throat. "I thought it might soothe things while we waited for Burning Elk."

"And you do look so much better than you did in the lobby, Molly, honest!" Audrey explained. "It was so scary when you passed out like you did. We didn't know what was happening. I mean, the hotel is off-limits for curses or jinxes, of course, so we knew it couldn't be that, so we thought maybe it was—"

"Why don't we let these two sort out just *what* it is, okay Audrey?" Jacobi broke in, knowing his daughter's love of and capacity for conversation.

"Oh, yes, sorry!" she said, heading for the door. "I'll get a thermos full of tea for you to take with you, Molly. Feel better!"

"Thank you, dear," Molly said.

164

Jacobi hugged Molly. "We're here if you need us," he said.

"Remember what you promised," Molly told him.

A look of sadness crossed Jacobi's face. It was only the third time Molly had ever seen him sad in their entire lives.

"I do. Juniper will be safe."

Jacobi left the room, leaving Burning Elk and Molly alone in it.

"If your wife finds out that we were in a hotel room alone together," Molly said dryly, "she's going to be displeased."

Burning Elk laughed a solid, loud laugh.

"You're right! Pela wouldn't make me any nalesniki for a month of Sundays!" he said, reaching into a pouch on a belt around his waist. He pulled out a small pipe and rubbed the end of it on his dirty jeans.

"Oh, no, I told you after last time, I'll never smoke with you again!" Molly said, pointing at him accusingly.

Burning Elk's smile faded. "I'm sorry, my girl, but I don't see any other way to sort out how you got somebody's extra in you."

Rodger

June 17, 1991

"Gaanzir gati, hamun iutu," Rodger spoke aloud the words he was taught as he smudged burning sage into his hand over a large, flat, purple crystal placed before him. The slightly overweight, jovial father of three years ago was gone. A gaunt scarecrow of a man with sunken eyes and a patchy beard had replaced him.

However, what Rodger had lost in weight had been replaced by knowledge. For instance, Rodger now knew that there were things in the dark. Creatures that reason could not comprehend. He'd crisscrossed the country, stealing what he needed after he'd run out of money, following the trail that would lead him to his lost daughter.

He'd returned to Timberhaven four months ago after discovering how to get to the place Melinda had been lost to.

The Pitch.

Eventually, as Rodger continued to speak, kneeling before his altar of stacked stones, animal skulls, and bird feathers, there was movement amongst his array of oddities. An owl feather shifted, and there, standing about two inches tall, stood the body of a mastodon, with an extended, wormlike tendril where a trunk should have been. The end of its tendril formed into the face of a screaming baby.

The creature, Veneswill, had appeared.

"You've brought my fee then?" the creature asked, its small voice all but lost over the sound of the wind, slipped from the mouth of the baby, still crying.

"I've got it," Rodger said. He pushed the purple crystal toward Veneswill.

The baby's face stopped crying, its wide eyes blinking away the tears as Veneswill took in the crystal, some three times bigger than Veneswill itself.

"Yes, this will serve my needs well," Veneswill giggled.

Rodger picked the crystal back up. "We had a deal. I get you this, you take me to your side."

"And I will," Veneswill said. "But it's not as easy as all that. You are man, made up of meat and bone. We Pitchborn consist of sterner stuff."

Rodger began to stand upright, the crystal still in hand.

"There's no need to be hasty," Veneswill's shouts sounded like angry bees to Rodger's ears as the Pitchborn reared back on its Mastodon legs. The baby's face was screaming again. "Our deal stands. Besides, with what you hold in your hand, I shall be able to claim a sole seat of power and grant the access you require to my realm."

Rodger sat back down and handed the crystal over.

Streetlights

On

Juniper

Juniper was freaked out. There was a monster loose and running through the woods surrounding her house, and that was something to freak out over. Jake walked along beside her, seemingly no worse for wear from the news. He just happily snacked on another fig.

Juniper needed to sit down. She found that being logical was much more comfortable for her if she was sitting while she thought about things. She found herself turning the box with her Tesla coil in it over and over in the front pocket of her hoodie.

"Juniper, it will be okay," Story said, peering out from the top of the backpack and purring in Juniper's ear.

Juniper sat down in a ditch at the side of the road. Jake walked a few more steps but then realized what she'd done and doubled back, sitting beside her.

"Do you have to chomp?" she asked briskly.

Jake swallowed and then threw the last bite of the fig into his mouth. "S'no good if you don' chomp it."

"Jake, we're in trouble here!" Juniper snapped. "What do we do? Slow is missing and may be dead, your brother and his friends are after us, and now there's a monster!"

Jake swallowed again. "There was a monster already," he said, counting off on his fingers, "Tod is always trying to get us, and," he scrunched up his face, "well, Slow missing is bad."

"Duh!" Juniper snapped again.

"Stop yelling!" Jake said, getting up and walking away.

"Where are you going?" Juniper chased after him.

"You keep yelling and not being nice to me." It looked to Juniper that Jake was going to cry.

Juniper ran up and got in front of Jake, stopping him.

"I'm sorry," she said. A thought occurred to her then, and she pulled the box out of her hoodie pocket. "Here," she said, opening the box all the way for the first time. "Check this out."

Jake peered at what she had as she put the now empty box back into her hoodie pocket. It looked kind of like a little tower with a hat on. "What is that?"

"Well, it's not a real one, but it's a Tesla coil! Watch this," Juniper's eyes lit up as she pushed the button at the base of the toy. The top of it spun and began to shoot out little yellow sparks.

Jake yelled and jumped away. "Don't, that will hurt!"

"No, Jake," Juniper explained, putting the toy up against her hand to show that the sparks were harmless. "See?"

"Stop!" Jake backed up further, his eyes growing wet.

Juniper put the toy into her pocket with its box and showed him her empty hand.

"I was just trying to make you feel better. I'm sorry, Jake, for real," she said as he wiped his eyes dry on his shirt sleeve and then wiped his nose with his arm.

"S'okay," he mumbled.

"No, it's not okay," Juniper explained. "I'm just scared, and I don't know what to do."

Jake looked at her. "What I was gonna say was that maybe we get Slow first, and then he can help us with the other parts. He's a big kid."

Juniper took a breath and patted Jake's shoulder. "That's good, Jake, it's a good idea. But we don't know where to find Slow. I haven't even figured out the clue we got yet." Juniper started them walking again.

"See, but," Jake ran around in front of Juniper this time. "Wait, *listen*," he stopped her. "We just need to find Jack."

Juniper didn't understand. "What are you talking about? Who's Jack?"

Jake shifted back and forth from one foot to the other, like someone who thinks they know the answer to a question but doesn't have the faith to go with their gut. "Well, in that book that your grandma gave me—that one you didn't want?

There's a guy in it named Jack, and he kills a bunch of giants. And the Cartoon Man—"

"Willoughby," Juniper interrupted.

"I know his name!" Jake yelled. "Willoughby, anyway, he said that we needed to see the giant killer. That's *Jack*!"

"So, you think we need that book?" Juniper asked.

"I hope not," Jake said sadly. "Tod tore it up when he found me reading it in the yard."

Juniper couldn't take it anymore. The pressure of being in charge was too much. She took off her backpack and lifted the flap up.

"What do we do, Story, I—"

But her backpack was empty.

"Where'd your cat go?" Jake asked before Juniper had the chance to.

Slow

Slow was up in a tree. He didn't know how he'd gotten up in a tree, but there he was anyway. He climbed to the top of it and looked around, finding himself deep in a forest. There was a half-moon light all around, though the sky had no moon or stars in it, just an empty blanket of midnight.

Slow kept his song going, thinking about it over and over as he climbed back down the tree. He climbed for what seemed like ages; the light from the moonless sky was long gone. He hadn't reached the ground.

Slow continued climbing down.

He climbed until his arms ached and his legs shook. Then he kept climbing.

Somewhere from way back in the back of his mind, a notion struck him.

Let go.

He thought he had heard it as if somewhere, out in the dark, someone had echoed that small thought out loud.

Let go.

Slow climbed down, lower and lower still.

Let go.

His body heaved with every breath.

Let go.

"I can't."

Let go.

Slow's foot shook, almost missing the next branch down.

Let go.

"I won't."

Let go.

It was so hard. Days passed. Without food, without water. Just endless climbing. Slow was hardly conscious of the climbing. His body was on automatic, repeating the motions.

Let go.

"I don't want to."

Let go.

"NO!"

And then Slow's feet touched the ground. His body hummed with exhaustion. His heart pounded. The tree he'd been climbing for so long was gone, and the entire forest with it. He was now in an open field. He laid down on the ground and looked up into the vast darkness above him, his song still playing in his head, his fingers, bloodied to a pulp, still playing the air, begging for Yvette. Slow closed his eyes and drew in a long, deep breath.

He coughed, and when he opened his eyes, Slow saw an old woman sitting by a campfire with a gray-haired coyote.

"Hello?" he called out.

The woman looked over and smiled. "Welcome," she said. "You must be another message, carved out of nothing."

The coyote bound over in one quick move to stand in front of Slow. It stared at him with yellow eyes and sniffed his bloody hands.

"Huh," the woman said. "The old man says no."

"Who are you?" Slow asked. "What is this place?" his voice started sounding like an echo—as if he was talking from miles off instead of a few yards away. The woman's voice started to be affected too. It began to cut in and out like bad reception on a television.

"I'm __ly." She said. "We're in the __ realm. It's quite dark here. Don't remember it always being so dark. Maybe I __ too much."

"I can't understand you," Slow yelled. He tried to walk closer to her, to her fire, but the coyote barred his path, snarling at him.

"Oh, better not," the woman said, looking at the coyote. "I don't know why, but __ doesn't want you to __ here."

"How do I get back?" Slow begged.

Slow could see a shimmering gray gossamer web float near the woman. Its tendrils slithered around like a slow-moving octopus.

"Look out!" he yelled, trying to point out the web to the woman.

She looked up in horror as the web descended on her face and neck, wrapping itself around her head completely.

The coyote snapped at Slow, still showing its teeth at him.

"Help her!" Slow yelled.

The woman moaned, unable to breathe as the scene filled with smoke. The coyote, for its part, backed away into the smoke, keeping an eye on Slow until it, too, sank into the cloud, and the entire area vanished back into the black.

A voice came, booming into Slow's head.

*You couldn't have helped, son; only got in the way. You're almost home now. Don't forget your song, and do **not** follow the stones. Their sparkle is not worth the trade. Remember what I said.*

But Slow, alone in his head once again, would not.

Rodger

September 18th, 1993

Rodger stopped writing in his notebook long enough to sip from the coffee mug before him. It had gone cold an hour ago, but he didn't seem to notice. What's more, he missed that the waitress was getting more annoyed each time she stopped by his booth.

"My shift ends soon," she huffed, scowling, as she placed his bill, *Coffee/.75,* on the table. "If that will be all."

"Freshen this up, please," Rodger said, immediately returning the pencil to the notebook without looking up.

The waitress snatched the mug up so quickly that some coffee spilled across the table. She mumbled as she walked back to the counter.

Rodger continued writing.

Veneswill, my devil deal-maker, the lesser of evils. I've helped him build his machine in exchange for access to The Pitch; maps, guides, and the like. He's reclaimed his monarchy these past few years, but I don't know that I'm any closer to my girl. How could I tell? Their rules are different there—reality as I know it doesn't mesh. Underneath, in the Pitch, where the hair and the vomit and the refuse of the world go, there stands a lone tower. At the top of the tower is a green, smokeless flame, a signal to Ancients who no longer see, nor do they care to, if they yet live. Acknowledgment of such a realm is unnecessary to such as they; better to forget the Pitch than to allow its existence to sully their paradigm.

But that does not serve the denizens of the Pitch.

No, it does not.

Oh yes, there be Pitchborn among that rabble, castoff from reality and forced to grow as rot does beneath a fallen branch.

The tower serves merely as a reminder to the Pitchborn that they are unwanted, and for that, they hate it. They have their hate and hunger. For all Pitchborn know hunger. It is what sustains them in the Pitch, in the Everdark. It lets them

know they exist, in a reality that would rather they did not.

Veneswill maintains a sense of order, such as it is, now

that their civil war has been quelled, and I search. Expedition

after expedition, looking for my Melinda. The Pitchborn claim

there's a danger in my coming back again and again, but no

matter. I'll break their world into a million pieces if it gets me

back my daughter. My little girl. Burn the rest of it.

The waitress slammed the coffee pot down on the table,

causing Rodger to jump back.

"Ya know, I saw you coming in the door," the waitress,

Ruby by her nametag, waved a finger at Rodger. "I thought *Oh,*

no. Another bum. Probably here looking for handouts. But I

brought you coffee anyhow. Did it with a smile, too, because

I'm a good Christian."

Rodger wiped the coffee drops off his freshly written

page and then put the notebook in his bag. He reached into his

front pocket and fished out a crumpled dollar bill, placing it on the table, carefully avoiding the spilled coffee. Then Rodger noticed that the sun that was rising when he got to the diner at dawn was nearly ready to set again. In updating his journal, time seemed to have gotten away from him.

"Apologies, ma'am," Rodger said, and then went out into the dusk.

Jake

Juniper was scared, Jake knew. He'd never seen her afraid before. But she wasn't as used to monsters as he was.

Jake knew monsters well.

Even at only six years old, Jake knew that the thing to do was to run away from monsters. It wasn't like in the movies. You didn't fight monsters yourself. You hid, or you went and got Juniper. Or Santa. But Jake was a little fuzzy on where the North Pole was. He figured it must be pretty far away, though, and Santa didn't have a phone.

Jake had mailed Santa a letter last year at Christmastime. He'd wished for Tod to be nice and for his mom to be at home more.

But neither of those things had happened.

Then Jake saw a cartoon about how boys and girls had to be good to get what they asked for from Santa.

So Jake was trying to be good. He stayed quiet at home, hidden away so that no one would notice he was there unless they called for him to do chores. When Jake couldn't get over to Juniper's house for meals, he ate berries and leaves from the forest around his house. Tod ate all the food at their house because he was the biggest.

Jake didn't mind so much. He liked berries.

But Juniper was scared, and she lost her cat, and Jake didn't know what to do. He wished Tod hadn't torn up the fairy book that Juniper's grandma had given Jake. That was the only giant killer he knew.

Jake and Juniper walked along a railroad. It was raised high so they could see to either side of them if anyone or anything was coming. It had been Juniper's idea. Jake thought she was the smartest person in the world. She'd figure out how to beat the monster and get Slow back from wherever he was. Jake just figured on keeping a watchful eye until Juniper found the answer.

He kept looking on either side of the tracks as they walked.

Finally, Juniper spun around and grabbed Jake by the shoulders.

"Jack!" she yelled. "Jake, you're a genius!"

Jake smiled a great big smile. He didn't know exactly what a genius was, but the way Juniper was acting, he thought it must be something great, like a hero or someone who wins a medal, so he liked being called one quite a lot.

"Willoughby even said 'in name if not in deed'!" Juniper continued cheering. "How could I not have put it together after you were so smart to answer the clue?"

"Yay!" Jake danced around, waving his arms like someone had filled them with jumping beans, still entirely unaware as to why he was cheering.

"So let's go find him before it gets dark out," Juniper grabbed Jake's hand and started them running.

Jake was confused. "But where are we going?"

"We've got to find Mr. Jack!" Juniper said, letting go of Jake's hand as they ran along the tracks.

Molly

The sky was bluish-gray, Molly knew, but she couldn't quite get it to look right as she came back to the reality she knew. Flat on her back in the middle of someone's garden, a lumpy potato sticking her in the back, Molly rubbed the fuzziness out of her eyes.

"I said I'd never do it again," she groaned, sitting up. It was getting to be nightfall, and she needed to get home to Juniper.

She opened her eyes once the world stopped spinning, only to find that Burning Elk was nowhere around.

"That son of a—"

"Careful how you paint me," Burning Elk said, coming from behind some bushes and adjusting his belt. "Else folks are bound to think you unladylike."

Molly stood up and made to charge Burning Elk.

"I'll show you unladylike! You've got me high as a kite in a garden and—"

Burning Elk grabbed Molly's arms and put his face up to hers.

"Stay upset, Molly, stay mad!" he said. "I need you to stay focused on what I'm saying."

Molly tried to shake him off. "You don't need to tell me to stay mad, and I can hear you just fine, you crazy old coot. Let go of me!"

Burning Elk held Molly tight, fighting her attempts to free herself and looking her in the eyes with his best calming look. Molly noticed concern in his eyes, and that made her worry. Had something happened while she was out there reliving her hippy days? What was it?

Juniper?

The fear crept up, forcing Molly to forget her anger at Burning Elk.

"Molly, no, no, no," Burning Elk said, shaking her.

Molly felt the sadness again, the sadness that was not her own. She began to cry.

"Burning Elk?" she wept, staring at him with sad, empty eyes save for the tears running down her face.

Burning Elk sat her down and then followed suit, pulling out a small wooden flute as he did. "Follow the song, Molly," he began to play.

Molly felt the sadness come over her body like a physical thing; a black sheet of tar that enveloped her from her feet to her head, coming down over her eyes.

The last thing she saw was the look in Burning Elk's eyes.

It was fear.

Juniper

The two children left the train tracks and ran for Kings Park, dodging people who were all headed home from the day's work or just frequenting shops in New Town.

"He was at the park earlier this afternoon," Juniper said between gasps of caught breath.

"Juniper," Jake said, panting. "Let's stop for a second, please?"

Juniper slowed down to a stop and put her hands on her knees, catching her breath as quickly as she could. Jake fell to the ground, too tired to care about people walking around him.

"We've got to go find him," Juniper said, looking in the direction of the park. "Come on, Jake, get up."

Jake stood up after much effort, and the two began to walk toward Kings Park. The street lights were coming on, an invitation for the night to come. Jake sighed.

"I am so dead," he said. "Juniper, I'm dead. Not only will Tod kill me, but my mom probably will be wanting to, too."

Juniper looked over and patted Jake on the shoulder.

"Don't worry, Jake, me and Molly will walk you home once we get everything sorted. We'll explain to your mom."

The crowd started to thin out the closer they came to Kings Park, just a teenage boy and girl who looked to be on a date and a couple of lost dogs who had taken residence inside the park. The dogs ran off when Jake tried to whistle them over.

"I don't see him anywhere," Juniper said, squinting around every corner of the park until, "Wait! There he is!"

She ran over to the bench where Mr. Jack was sitting and enjoying a scone, his purple bowler hat there beside him.

"Mr. Jack, Mr. Jack!" Juniper and Jake both yelled.

"Mr. Jack, you've gotta help, quick!" Jake yelled the last part.

"My word, children," Mr. Jack said worriedly, standing before them. "Whatever the predicament is, I'm sure we can overcome it. You need only to calm down and talk."

Jake just pointed to Juniper, who took the lead.

"We need your help, Mr. Jack," she began. "We can't find our friend, Slow. Remember? You met him with me this afternoon."

Mr. Jack rubbed his head, remembered his bowler hat, and retrieved it from the bench. He then gave Jake his leftover scone after he saw Jake's mouth water at the sight of it.

"Start from the beginning, Ms. Soot," Mr. Jack said.

Slow

The sounds of a city were all around Slow, yet the city he was in stood empty to his eyes. He could only *hear* life there. It pulsed through the streets and buildings around him like lifeblood, pumping a steady course of noise and vibrations from an unseen source.

Slow walked, as he had been for what seemed like years. He vaguely remembered Cal's Bar, recalling events there like some dream he'd had while half-awake. Even Twist, the only reason he made it out of that bar, seemed like a scuffed charcoal drawing in his mind's eye.

The walking and his song, those were his constants.

His True North.

Time wasn't even a constant here. He felt it pass by, leaving him as an afterthought. A guitarist out of Boston—an old-timer—once told Slow that Time makes a friend of no man. The best you can hope for is a civil acquaintance.

But here, even Time wasn't civil to Slow. Had he only been fifteen when he started walking? He found it hard to believe. He missed Yvette. The arthritis he felt in his hands wasn't enough to keep his fingers from remembering the feel of her. He strummed the air in reminiscence as his knees wobbled unsurely. They preferred the soft ground of the country or the sandy beaches to the hard sidewalks of cities.

Slow had walked for so long.

He'd seen the first creature coming out of a barbershop, its gray, flaccid skin sagging all over its body like too much meat dangling from a sandwich. He saw hundreds more almost immediately after seeing the first one. They were everywhere. He saw them working a ticket window at the theater and planting a small window booth garden outside of an apartment building. Though they wore no clothes, they were human-sized creatures with earthworm heads and grub-like fleshy bodies, which is how he ended up with his name for them.

Grubs.

The Grubs were the things that finally gave Slow an answer to the noise he heard, the city life. He didn't know why he couldn't see them before, but that time was over. He was in their town, walking their streets, breathing their air.

For the most part, they, in turn, seemed oblivious to him. They simply lived their lives without paying him the slightest notice.

It was like Slow didn't exist.

Three months after seeing his first Grub, Slow noticed the mouth of the tunnel, wondering how he could have ever missed it during his crisscrossing of the city. It gaped like a hungry baby in between two high-rise buildings, an explosion of basketball-sized white quartz scattered around its entrance. He walked to its lip and peered down its depths until the darkness inside swallowed his vision some fifty feet down. The walls of the tunnel were black and smooth, making Slow wonder where the white stones had come from.

He took an exploratory step toward the entrance and ran his fingers along its carved, even wall. "Hello?" he called down the tunnel. He didn't sound the way he had remembered sounding. His voice, ragged from lack of use, reminded him of a grandfather's and not his own.

Two of the white stones began to roll about Slow's feet, quietly circling him like hungry sharks. At each rotation, each tumble, however, Slow noticed that the stones seemed to glow; a soft, green light emanated from them.

The stones stopped their rumbling around and quickly dashed down the tunnel.

"What was—" Slow asked, bewildered.

Slow turned around to find that a small group of Grubs had collected behind him, their eyeless faces pointed in his direction.

"Hello?" he said, trying to gauge a reaction, some sign that they were, in fact, noticing him.

As one, the group of Grubs tilted its heads slightly to one side like curious dogs. They stepped forward toward Slow, first one small step, then another.

"Can you hear me?" Slow asked, backing up. "Do you understand me?"

More Grubs came, from out of and around the nearby buildings and from the street, to join the mob before Slow; all with loose, almost marionette-like movements; with fleshy, gray heads tilted on blubbery necks. The Grubs began to surround Slow in the alley.

He turned to the cavern's mouth, the faint glow of the stones barely still visible inside. Slow ran toward it, down into the dark.

Jake

It wasn't that Jake was disinterested in the telling of Juniper's tale to Mr. Jack (Jake was a co-star in the story, after all.) And he certainly hadn't meant to overhear what he had overheard, but anyone would have been distracted by three dogs arguing over the best way to kidnap and make away with a small child, *particularly* if the person doing the overhearing was, in fact, a small child.

"Juniper," Jake said, tugging on the sleeve of Juniper's hoodie.

"Not now, Jake," Juniper explained, "I'm almost to the part with the monster."

"Monster?" Mr. Jack's face went white.

"But, over there, by that other bench—" Jake started, pointing.

"Yes, Mr. Jack, that's when a monster ate Jake's pants." Juniper continued, interrupting Jake with her story.

The three dogs were all different breeds—one large black (what Juniper, who had read many books about dogs, would have told him was a Mastiff, had she been paying attention), one mid-sized brown (a German short-haired Pointer), and one small gray (a Scottish Terrier), were converged on the bench that Jake had tried pointing out to Juniper. The medium and large dogs were seated in front of it while the small dog walked back and forth in front of them on the bench. Before Jake knew exactly what he was doing, he had wandered over to get within better earshot, hiding behind a bush.

"It's not like I don't think it's a swell plan, Whisper," the large black dog said, "I just don't know if it'll be that easy."

"It's not for the likes of you to wonder now, is it?" the small dog, Whisper, replied, "I'm in charge of this task, so I'll be making the plans that you'll be adhering to."

"Yeah, Shadow," the mid-sized dog turned to the big black, "listen to the boss. She's in charge."

"Nobody likes you, you know." Shadow said, turning to the medium brown in reply, "It's well known that Row is a butt sniffer and not of any noble dogline."

Row growled at Shadow then, his tail sticking straight out. With a snort, Shadow turned and stood up, towering over Row.

"Enough!" Whisper said, jumping between them, "Will I need to tell The Emperor of Refuse that he wasted his favors on we three? That because a Brute and a Middling couldn't, nay, *wouldn't* listen to my instructions, the instructions of an Emperor-appointed Short, I might add, we were unable to capture and return with a sole Pitchborn?"

Shadow sat back down, and Row quieted.

"There will be no need to tell Lord Veneswill anything." Shadow began, "I will do as you say. Stick to your plan."

"Let it not be said that Row was unwilling to follow where a Short did lead." Row bowed.

Whisper sighed, finding both dogs in her company tiresome. She would need to see about hiring better as soon as the opportunity presented itself.

"As I was saying," she began again, "Agares is said to have planted Claptrap here using a small child, Shadow. It is known. So, we grab a child of our own to use as bait to draw Claptrap out, and we'll be nearly there." She nodded to the large black, "Have no fear. All is going according to plan."

Jake, too interested in what he was seeing and hearing, didn't pay enough attention to how far he was leaning forward. He snapped through the bush like an angry elephant. The three dogs bound over to him and stood over Jake before he knew what to do.

"Oh, um, hello, talking dogs," Jake said, looking up at them.

"He heard us!" Row said, growling.

"Shall I dispose of him?" Shadow asked Whisper, showing Jake his sharp, white teeth.

"What's 'dispose' mean?" Jake asked. He wasn't scared. He'd seen bigger, scarier teeth earlier in the day.

"It means dead." Row laughed.

Jake tried to look over and see if Juniper was coming to help, but the small dog jumped onto his back as soon as he moved. He winced as her tiny claws dug into his skin through his shirt.

"Kill?!" Whisper barked at her underlings, "This is what we were looking for! Bait, remember?" She jumped off Jake just long enough for the other two dogs to slump him over Shadow's back.

"Sorry, Whisper," Row looked down guiltily. "I was just caught up in the moment."

"Yeah, apologies," Shadow grunted as Jake shifted a bit on his back.

"Payday may come early this time, boys," Whisper sighed as the three made their way back through the brush at the edge of the park and into the woods.

Timberhaven

Nickie Fraser tended the bar at The Pub between semesters at UMKC Medical School, which is why Essa sought her out.

Essa pulled Nickie into the office, where the med student saw a striking red-headed woman, Brynne Dusayer, kneeling by the side of the unconscious figure of a young man, no more than a teen, soaking wet and laid out on the couch. "Is he—"

"He's not dead," Brynne interrupted. Nickie didn't know if she believed the local hubbub about Brynne being psychic, but the redhead often interrupted people, answering questions before people asked them. Nickie chalked it up to Brynne being perceptive. "But I think his time is short."

"Then we need to call 911!" Nickie yelled

"Now, there's no need for that," Essa said, shushing Nickie in a slight German accent that she's never lost, no matter how many miles or years removed. "We've got him breathing again, you see. I only wondered if you couldn't check his, you know, they are called, oh, his necessaries."

"His necessaries?" Nickie asked.

"Vitals," Brynne said.

"Oh," Nickie walked over, shaking her head, and placed her index and middle finger at the boy's wrist. "Pulse is strong." She lifted his eyelids. "Pupils aren't dilated. What's going on, Essa?"

Essa pulled her long black hair back into a clip, keeping it out of her face as she took a seat in a chair by the young man's head. Nickie marveled at the young woman's physique, even in a tense moment like they'd found themselves. Nickie was twenty-seven years old. Essa was at least pushing fifty, given the time that Nickie had known her, yet Nickie looked the older of the two.

Essa lit a tall, blue candle and set it on the coffee table next to her at the young man's side.

"There is trouble," Essa said. "If this boy's body is safe

for now, could you let Gerald know I will be late in coming

down to run the bar this evening?"

Juniper

Juniper immediately noticed that Jake was not there once she finished telling Mr. Jack their story. She had turned to him to ask, "Isn't that right, Jake," since it was, after all, his story too, and he was gone.

"Jake!" Juniper yelled, "Jake!"

"Now, let us not fret, my child," Mr. Jack said absently, as though preoccupied with a faraway dream, "I'm sure he was just here not a moment ago."

"But, there was—the monster, Mr. Jack, it was after Jake before. What if it got him?"

"Where's my brother, Junkyard?" Tod skidded in front of the pair, nearly hitting Juniper. Curtis and Bobby were close behind him. Tod hopped off his bike and pushed Juniper, grabbing a hold of her backpack as he spun her out of it.

"Now see here, ruffian!" Mr. Jack shouted, standing between Tod and Juniper.

Tod swung a fist at Mr. Jack, hitting him square in the face. Mr. Jack toppled backward onto the ground.

"Think I won't hit a psycho?" Tod said as he dug through Juniper's backpack. Curtis snickered from five feet behind them.

Juniper ran over to Mr. Jack, who had curled up and held his bloodied nose. She looked frantically around the park for any help at all. She found none coming.

"Just leave us alone," Juniper pleaded to the group of boys, almost whispering.

"'Just leave us alone.'" Curtis mocked her. Bobby smiled. After emptying her backpack of a pair of pants and a figs package, Tod threw it down and walked over to her. He grabbed Juniper by a fistful of hair and stood her up before him.

"Where's," he flicked Juniper in the forehead, "my," flick, "brother?" flick.

"You told him to go home," Juniper said, trying to wriggle free, "he's probably at your house!"

Tod punched Juniper in the stomach, knocking the breath from her. He threw her to the ground. Juniper tried to suck air in, but she was left gasping.

Suddenly there was a twerp-cheep from a police car on the road, its red and blue lights spinning.

"Tod, cops!" Bobby shouted, "Scatter!" and he rode away on his bike with Curtis pedaling right behind. Tod grabbed his bike and rode away, shouting, "You know the deal, Junkyard, your grandma's dead!"

Juniper lay in the grass, crying and still unable to breathe.

Mr. Jack came to her, his hand to his nose with an orange handkerchief.

"Juniper?" he asked worriedly, shouting to the police car, "Here! Come, this child needs aid!"

Juniper could hear the jangling of keys, and someone was talking on a radio. She rolled onto her stomach, finally able to take a breath to see the shoes of Deputy Barnhart.

"Is she okay?" he asked.

"Of course she isn't!" Mr. Jack announced through gritted teeth, "Does she appear to be okay? Assist her."

Deputy Barnhart helped Juniper stand up.

"Where's Jake?" Juniper worried, looking around to nearby bushes.

"What's going on here?" Deputy Barnhart asked, "Was that Tod Steadherd and his two idiots?"

"I should say it was indeed." Mr. Jack explained.

"Were they picking on you?" the deputy asked Juniper.

"'Picking on her?'" Mr. Jack scowled, "They *beat* the child! They hit *me*!"

"*What's going on, Ollie?*" came a voice over the walkie-talkie at Deputy Barnhart's hip.

"Well, Sheriff, we've got Molly's grandchild here in the park with, um, *Mr. Jack*." Deputy Barnhart replied on his radio. Juniper thought the way he said Mr. Jack's name was strange. "It seems I'll need to stop by the Steadherd residence after I get her back to Molly."

"*Is she okay? Is she hurt?*" the Sheriff's voice came back.

"Bruised up a bit." the deputy returned, "Seems more scared than anything."

"*Well, Tod's done it this time. I don't care that his mom's an old friend.*" the Sheriff growled, "*Take her on home, Ollie, and then radio me when you get to the Steadherd place.*"

"Will do, Sheriff." the deputy hooked his walkie-talkie back onto his belt. "Let's get you home to your grandma, little one; I bet she's worried." He turned to Mr. Jack, "I'll handle things from here, sir."

"Juniper," Mr. Jack knelt in front of Juniper, "you should go on with the deputy. I'll look for Jake." He stood back

211

up and put his hands on her shoulders, "We'll sort all of this out, you'll see."

Juniper looked all around the park.

"But you were supposed to have the answer." Juniper said, "You were going to tell us how to find Slow. I don't understand."

"Come on," the deputy guided Juniper by her shoulder toward the squad car, "it's getting dark out, and we should all just head on home."

"I'll find him!" Mr. Jack yelled to Juniper, "I'll get Jake home safely!"

First Slow, then Story, and now Jake. Juniper was starting to feel all alone. She watched as the sun set entirely, leaving Timberhaven draped in night.

And she shivered.

Molly

Molly opened her eyes.

She was sitting in an empty field. The sun was rising. The wind caressed the grass around her into gentle waves of brown and gold as the whole blue sky looked down at her like a watchful parent. Molly stood up and, in doing so, noticed the dress she was wearing. A simple dress hung loosely from her shoulders as it billowed around her body in the breeze.

Molly looked around, taking in her surroundings. She wasn't anywhere that she recognized. She took a few steps, barefoot in the grass, and began to turn, looking to the horizon. Molly thought for merely the flash of a second that she saw someone standing in a line of trees at the edge of her sight, but it was too far away to be sure.

"Who are you, and why are you here?" came a man's voice from behind Molly, startling her.

She spun around, nearly tripping over her own feet, to find no one was there.

"Wh-who's there?" she asked the wind, though she could hear someone walking around her in the grass.

"*Edvard Grieg.*" the voice responded.

Molly turned again, this time catching sight of a man with dark hair with flashes of silver at his forehead and temples, dressed in a brown suit with tails, his hands in his front pockets, walking away. Molly ran to catch him.

"Edvard? I'm," she began, sidestepping a tricky patch of thorns as she went, "I'm Molly Matheson and I—"

"**I'm** *not Edvard Grieg,*" the man in the suit interrupted, "*but we are currently walking through his piece.*"

"I don't understand," Molly said, matching the man's step. "Where is this place? Where's Burning Elk?"

"**Morning Mood,** *it would seem.*" the man continued as though Molly hadn't spoken, "*Lucky for us, it's not the Mountain King, eh? Nothing worse than outmaneuvering trolls before one's had a proper breakfast.*"

"What?" Molly shook her head, terribly perplexed.

"I'd say you're more confused than perplexed. Befuddled, maybe, but that's a descriptor that isn't fully understood by many these days. Besides, they're all so similar it doesn't matter in any case."

"I didn't—" Molly stopped walking.

"No, no, I know you didn't." the man said, turning around to face Molly, *"Never mind. I'd like to be on my way, but it seems that will not happen until we play this scene out."*

"W-what?" Molly stuttered.

"This will go much more quickly if you stop saying that. Incidentally, my name is Calithan. Some call me Cal, but I'd rather you didn't." He turned and started them walking through the field again, headed toward the trees in the distance.

"I'm Molly—"

"Matheson, yes, you've said that already. Let's see if I can speed this along." Calithan walked around a large indentation in the grass, maybe a lounging place for a deer or a cow, *"So, Molly, you're here, but you don't know how you got*

215

here or where here is. You've lost track of Burning Elk, or, more likely, he's lost track of you, and—admittedly, this is merely an assumption on my part—you'd like to get back home. Have I left anything out?"

Molly was quietly thinking over and absorbing everything Calithan said.

"I'll take your silence to mean that I haven't." Calithan retorted over his shoulder. *"So, now we just need to figure out what kind of story you're having."*

"Story?"

"Yes, story. Every story is an event. Conversationally, however, not every event is a story."

"Nothing you say makes sense," Molly said, shaking her head and trying to catch up with Calithan's fast pace.

"I typically don't talk this much, but it seems you've caught me on a verbose day. I do love Grieg, which is all I have so far as an explanation." Calithan slowed a step so that Molly could catch up. The two walked side by side.

"So, what story I'm having. How will knowing that help anything?"

"It gives you a direction to go. For instance, if you are in a thriller—though, you'd doubtfully be dressed like that." Calithan gestured to Molly's dress.

"What's wrong with how I'm dressed?"

"Nothing's wrong, but it doesn't suggest a thriller. That's all." Calithan grabbed a weed as they walked by it, uprooting it and sticking it in his mouth, chewing on the end, *"Now, maybe a mystery."*

"Well, I certainly don't know what's going on, so let's start there." Molly decided, "Okay, I'm having a mystery. What now?"

Calithan thought about it for a few yards. *"I suppose I would be the Stranger, then."*

"Stranger? How do you mean?" Molly asked.

"In a mystery, the Stranger comes in and moves things along when the protagonist needs help. Somewhat deus ex machina, really, and not terribly original."

Molly was growing annoyed, "So sorry to be unoriginal. Wait a minute, how do you know that *I'm* not the stranger in *your* tale?"

"That's not possible. You see, the Witnesses are privy to what you've *been doing before now. They have no idea what I was doing before bumping into you in this field. Ergo, this is your story. Or, at least partially yours, but definitely not mine."*

Witnesses? Molly wondered to herself. She started to ask but immediately realized that she'd forgotten what it was she was about to ask about, so instead shook her head, "Fine. So, what's next?"

"Well," Calithan said as they reached the edge of the field and stepped into the forest, *"now we'll need to point you in the direction of your body. Wherever it is."*

Slow

Slow hurried his pace as his heart pounded.

Every time the stones would go around a bend, their soft light lost to him, swallowed up by the cavern, Slow would begin to pant and stumble along quickly until they were in sight again.

Slow figured it had been twenty minutes or so since he'd been surrounded by the Grubs up on the street. He wasn't entirely sure that going underground had been a rational choice, but it was the only option he'd had at the time.

He played his song again on the open air.

Once more, he longed for Yvette.

Sometimes the cave walls seemed to pulse—almost gently vibrating, causing Slow to need to reach out and feel them. It was odd, he thought, but the sound of the small, glowing rocks, rolling in guidance to him, made noises as rocks rolling across rocks *would* make, only the walls didn't feel like stone.

They felt softer. Like maybe Slow wasn't in a cave at all but rather an unfinished carnival maze with plywood walls covered in foam. Slow knelt to the ground at his feet and touched it.

"Huh. Now that feels like rock," he said.

Suddenly, the rolling rocks stopped and glowed more brightly, so much so that Slow was forced to cover his eyes.

"Hello? Who's there?" a voice called from somewhere in the tunnel ahead.

Slow didn't respond at first. It had been so long since he'd heard a voice outside his own that he didn't know what it was; he had forgotten how to converse.

"Who is it?" called the voice.

"Slow. Winslow Perkins." He answered, lowering his hand from his eyes as the light from the stones dimmed. He saw a man standing before him. The man looked rough, and not just because Slow was seeing him in dim green light in a cavern underground. His skin was deathly pale; his eyes were small and dark. Dressed in a long-sleeved dress shirt that was torn and frayed in many spots, he was dirty, with dark, unkempt hair, and barefoot, from what Slow could tell.

He quickly moved up to Slow and took his hand, grasping it in a handshake.

"Oh, praise be!" the man yelled as Slow tried to take his hand back, "It's been so long that I've been walking here. I-I had nearly given up hope of ever seeing another soul!"

Slow stepped back to look at the man more closely. Decades of travel since Cal's Bar had made him cautious.

"Who are you?" Slow asked the ragged man.

"Of course! Where are my manners? I'm Collin, Collin's my name." the man replied, fussily trying to make his threadbare clothes more presentable. "I'm sorry; I didn't look like this when I first arrived here."

Slow looked down at his old, arthritic hands. "No, me either."

"Lucky you've got these stones for light. I've been feeling my way in the dark."

The rocks started to roll forward again, down the cavern tunnel. Slow walked to keep up with them, planning to leave Collin where he stood.

"Wait!" the man yelled, "Can't I please come with you? We needn't talk; if that's to your liking, it's just, I'm afraid I'll go mad." Collin only whispered the last part, but Slow caught it. "And, I think I may have heard a way out of these caves! Only I didn't have the means to find it. Let me think, let me think," Collin paced, running his hands through his hair, "it was a tunnel some way back. With your light, we could…"

Slow fingered the notes to his song in the dank air of the cave and thought things over.

"We get out of these caves," he finally said, "and that's it. After, you go your way; I'll go mine."

Collin smiled a huge smile, nearly laughing, "Of course, of course. You're a man set in your ways. I can respect that."

The pair began to walk together, following the light of the rolling stones.

Jake

Typically, being in the forest near dark time scared Jake to no end, but Jake had found peace around dogs for as long as he could remember; always felt comfortable around them. So, even after finding himself bound and flung over the back of the big black dog named Shadow, Jake felt no fear. It was as though he were on an adventure out of a storybook, the stories that Juniper didn't like but that Jake loved. Where the heroes were tested, sometimes even bloodied, but as long as they stayed true, they always triumphed against whatever monsters they fought in the end. Good *always* won.

Jake wished it was that way in real life.

But still, he thought that dogs were generally good company.

Even if they had tied him up and ran off with him.

Jake shivered as the temperature dropped with the setting sun. He told himself it was because of the cold and not because he was scared of toothy monsters. Besides, he was with dogs.

"Where are we going?" he asked as the group made their way around a copse of beech trees that were grown too closely together to walk through.

"Quiet, boy," the dog named Row barked, "or I'll bite out your tongue."

"I only wondered, is all," Jake said, shrinking back as best he could. He found it difficult to do while being tied up.

"Leave him be." Whisper, the small gray dog growled, "And be quiet." Row glared up at Jake but let the matter go. Shadow laughed. "Besides," Whisper added, "we've got no idea if this is even going to work the same, using this boy instead of a girl."

"He is the right size," Shadow added. "The Emperor's specifications went no further than that."

"Except to say that the child used to trap Claptrap here was a *she*!" Whisper shrieked, turning to stare down Shadow.

The larger dog finally looked down, just as Row had before. It was Row's turn to laugh. Shadow growled and made to bite him but stopped when Whisper held her paw up suddenly.

"Shh!" she hissed, "There's something out there, in the bushes. Damned, we've not set the trap properly!"

"I smell it, too." Row said. Shadow nodded.

"I don't smell anything," Jake whispered, remembering the monster. "There's a monster around here. Lots of teeth and —"

"Shadow, if the whelp speaks again," Whisper said, her jaw clenched, "gag him."

Row looked up at Jake and laughed. Shadow promptly kicked the smaller dog in the ribs before turning his head back toward Jake.

"Best keep it quiet now, boy." the large dog said.

Jake did as he was told, looking around into the trees as best he could. It was getting darker inside the forest. The sun was all but down.

"Shadow," Whisper said, "set the child down—slowly —and get ready. This Pitchborn is notoriously tricky. Row," she gestured to the smaller of her two compatriots. "Flank to the left. Eyes up, everyone."

Jake wondered what would happen if the monster appeared again, just as the bushes ahead of him and his canine travelers exploded with movement.

He didn't need to wonder any longer.

Juniper

Juniper sat quietly as she rode away from Kings Park in Deputy Barnhart's patrol car, watching as Mr. Jack walked around calling out Jake's name. Juniper didn't know what to think. Slow was still missing, and they'd followed Willoughby's stupid clues, and it had gotten them nowhere. Now Story was gone, Jake was missing, and she was being taken back home to Molly, who would probably just be crying or making another tuna casserole.

Juniper sighed. She had no idea what she was going to do next, deciding that looking through Molly's books at home for more clues would be her only recourse. She focused on the blinking lights and computer equipment inside the police car as they drove on.

"You're gonna be okay, kid." Deputy Barnhart told her. Juniper didn't like being called *kid* by him. It made her think of Slow.

"Yeah." was all she replied.

"And I'll go handle Tod Steadherd just as soon as I get you home." Deputy Barnhart continued, smiling a great big smile, "I'll see to it that he won't bother you anymore."

"N-no, that's okay." Juniper jumped, "Really, there isn't any need to get Tod into any trouble. It was all a big misunderstanding." She grabbed Deputy Barnhart's coat sleeve. "Please, don't."

Deputy Barnhart's smile faded as he tried to understand Juniper's reaction.

"Well, I'm sorry, darlin', but that boy needs tending to." he looked back up, keeping his eyes on the road, "We can't have him accosting people in parks, and lord knows what else."

Juniper's panicky hands found the Tesla coil box inside her sweatshirt pocket. She put the toy back inside and began to flip it over and over again.

"I just don't think you have to, is all." she explained, "I'm getting home safely and—"

"I can appreciate that you're scared of the boy, hon, but I've got a job to do." Deputy Barnhart interrupted, talking over Juniper, "Don't you worry your pretty head about it, I'll see to it that he leaves you alone."

With that, they pulled up in front of Juniper's house, and Deputy Barnhart stopped the car, leaving it running. Any further argument that Juniper had so far as Tod was concerned was silenced once Deputy Barnhart got out and shut his door. He headed around to Juniper's side and opened hers.

"I'm going to make sure everything's okay here; maybe talk to your grandma a little bit." Deputy Barnhart said as Juniper got out, clutching her empty backpack to her.

As the two walked up the driveway toward the front door, Juniper noticed that every light in the house was on, from the attic window to the laundry room in the basement. The all too familiar smell of tuna casserole wafted out when Molly burst out the front door.

"There she is!" she yelled, her hands untying an apron from around her waist, "Where have you been, young lady?" Juniper was quite confused as Molly hugged her tightly.

"There was an incident in Kings Park, ma'am." Deputy Barnhart said with a reassuring smile, "But we'll take care of things from here. I just wanted to see the little lady home. I'll be off now that I see she'll be looked after."

"Well, of course, she'll be looked after!" Molly yelled, hugging Juniper tighter, "It's not like her to run off like this."

Juniper pushed away from her grandmother. Molly's behavior wasn't right. Something was off. Molly looked hurt as Juniper took a further step back.

"Well, okay, you run along inside, honey. I've made your favorite."

Juniper just stood and stared, not knowing what to do. There was an uncomfortable feeling crawling up Juniper's neck. That feeling of someone having been in your room, digging around in your things, only they didn't put things back exactly as you'd left them.

"Go on, darlin', do as your grandma says." Deputy Barnhart told the statue that was Juniper.

"Grandma?" Molly said, turning to the officer with eyes wide in disbelief, "Is that supposed to be funny?"

"Ma'am?" Deputy Barnhart seemed completely confused.

"Melinda, go inside and set the table. I'm going to have a word with the officer." Molly was talking to Juniper, but her eyes never left Deputy Barnhart.

"Wh-who's Melinda?" Juniper asked, taking another step back toward the house's front door.

"No time for games, Melinda honey, go inside while I finish up out here. I've got a piping hot dish of tuna casserole for you." Molly said, turning to Juniper this time.

"I hate tuna casserole, and my name's not Melinda!" Juniper yelled as she ran to the house, tears filling her eyes.

"Melinda!" Molly yelled after her, "Melinda!"

Juniper locked the front door behind her and ran upstairs to her room. She watched from her window as a very confused Deputy Barnhart got into his patrol car and drove away.

"Melinda!" Molly screamed, pounding on the front door. "Let me in right now, please. Melinda!"

Upstairs in her room, Juniper climbed into bed and hid her head under her pillow, trying to block out whoever was screaming at her in Molly's voice.

Timberhaven

"No, sir, I understand." Deputy Barnhart spoke into his radio, "I've left the Matheson house now and am en route to the Steadherd residence." He drove his police cruiser down the quiet street as the last rays of sun began to creep beneath the horizon.

"*I'll go check on Molly tomorrow.*" Sheriff Vindego's voice came from the radio in return, "*Sounds like things might be a little rough for her right now, with a little one thrust on her. You say she just started screaming?*"

Deputy Barnhart made the left on Sycamore toward Tod Steadherd's house. He was happy to deal with this punk, feeling as though the sheriff should have handled this situation long ago. Thinking how things would be different if he were sheriff.

"Yeah, she just started yelling 'Melinda' and trying to get back inside the house." Deputy Barnhart sighed, "Didn't you say—I thought the kid's name was June something."

"*Juniper, yeah.*" Sheriff Vindego returned, "*I don't know what's going on with that. Anyhow, come back in once you've finished at Denise—at the Steadherd place.*"

"Will do, over and out." Deputy Barnhart said, finishing just as he pulled into the Steadherd driveway.

Things seemed quiet in the house. He turned his lights on, spinning red and blue explosions into the dark forest that surrounded the scene. The house was completely dark as well, with not even a porch light on. The deputy got out of the car and walked up to the front door, knocking loudly on it.

"Police, open up!" he bellowed in his most serious, this means business voice.

When no one answered, he pounded again, bouncing the screen door and rattling it loudly. Still, as far as he could see, no lights came on in the house. He stepped from the porch into a poorly tended garden area, narrowly dodging an old, exploded box of fireworks that never got collected from the front yard.

"This place is a dump." Deputy Barnhart said under his breath.

He made his way around the side of the house, looking for signs that anyone was home. Finally, he came to the backyard. He brought a discarded trash can upright, and that's when he noticed that the back door to the house was open.

"Sheriff," he spoke into the radio.

"*Go ahead.*" Sheriff Vindego replied.

"Yeah, uh, there may be trouble here at the Steadherd place."

"*How do you mean?*"

"Well, the back door is busted and wide open for one. Place is dark. Quiet. I'm gonna go in and check things out."

"*Standby, Ollie, I'll be right there.*"

Deputy Barnhart walked up the steps to the open door. "Hello? This is the police." He raised his voice for the last part, "I'm coming in."

The house was quiet, outside of the broken glass from the door crunching under his feet. He could make out features in the kitchen thanks to the blue light from an ancient microwave that blinked *1:37*. Each step that Deputy Barnhart took in the empty house seemed to creak very loudly. He felt—he couldn't quite put his finger on it. Creeped out. The hair on his neck was standing up, too, which he didn't think happened in real life, but there it was.

"Hello, police!" he yelled, the unnatural fear he felt getting the better of him.

He walked into the living room, brandishing a flashlight and yelling again. No answer came except the radio at his hip.

"Ollie, dammit, I'm five minutes out. Wait for me." the sheriff's voice repeated.

A nightmare of shimmering teeth flashed in the light Deputy Barnhart was providing. It happened suddenly; one second, he was holding his flashlight. The next, his flashlight was lying on the ground, though his hand—bone and tendon sticking out at the wrist where it'd been bitten off—was still holding it tightly.

"Sh-sh-shi," he stuttered, feeling at the end of his bloody stump arm and tripping back toward the kitchen as he tried to locate what had attacked him in the dark room. But he couldn't find it, the thing that bit off his hand. It was in the dark, though, that much he could tell.

He could hear it moving. Hiding. Coming for him.

"*Ollie, answer me!*" came the sheriff once more from the radio.

Whatever was in the room with Deputy Barnhart attacked then, and Ollie did answer.

In screams.

Molly

Molly, no stranger to bizarre undertakings, admitted to herself that traipsing through a forest she didn't know with a man of Calithan's reputation was probably not the wisest course of action. However, she couldn't think of a better one given her circumstances.

"I know who you are, by the way." She said, pulling her dress free from a shrub as they walked.

Calithan's pace didn't slow as he navigated the forest floor. "*Which means you've heard stories about me.*"

Molly caught the two steps she'd lost in the bramble back up, returning to her position by his side.

"Your mood has certainly changed. Terse, and not overly friendly."

"*My mood, as you say, had changed before. Now it has simply reverted to form.*" Calithan stepped around a small trench. "*Mind the ditch.*"

Molly hopped over it, and a momentary flash of memory from her childhood crossed her mind, of leaping onto and over giant hay bales as she and her friends played in freshly mowed fields. She hadn't felt so much like herself in a long time.

"So it was the Grieg talking before?" she smiled.

"*As I had suggested it was.*" He returned, not smiling.

"Fine," Molly harrumphed, "be that way. Where are you taking me, anyway?"

"*As we've already established, I'm leading you in the direction of your body, so you can get back to your…I want to say, niece? Or was it a cousin?*" Calithan wondered, not looking at Molly. "*The girl, Julep.*"

"*Juniper* is her name, and she's my granddaughter," Molly said. She turned a menacing squint at Calithan. "And just how do you know about her? What is all of this?"

Calithan still didn't look at Molly, but said, "*Juniper, that's right. You see, Molly, I may have been a trifle misleading before. I'm familiar with the story you've currently found yourself in. It could be argued that I had a part to play in its prelude—albeit a small, nearly forgettable role—that I'm sure will be brought into the light at some point in the tale's telling.*"

"You're not making sense again," Molly rolled her eyes.

"*Be that as it may,*" Calithan continued, not slowing a step as he talked. "*Due to my acknowledging a measure of, let's call it, an obligation to your plight, I'm helping you in your quest. Presuming, of course, that you want to get back to your granddaughter.*"

"Now, you listen here," Molly stopped walking, planted her feet, and put her hands on her hips. "Of *course,* I want to get back to Juniper. What an ignorant thing to say. I love that little girl. I'd *die* for the kid!"

"*So you say,*" Calithan said, not turning around.

"Calithan!" Molly yelled.

At this, Calithan did stop and turned around.

"*You people*," he said. Molly could see, then, a storm setting in his eyes. "*Always opening with the sacrifice play. As if that level of melodrama means something more. As if your granddaughter wouldn't rather have you* live *for her,* with her, than to be left alone again."

"That's not what I—" Molly began, but Calithan turned away from her again.

Molly couldn't form words for a moment. She merely ground her teeth and took a deep breath through her nose. Finally, she took up after Calithan once more.

The pair continued walking in silence. Though there was no path to walk on—and it seemed to Molly like no human had ever set foot in that forest—they were keeping a quick pace. The trees surrounding them were old and gigantic, in that order, with roots that peeked up through the ground like craggy fingers. Sounds of life surrounded them; some Molly recognized: a toad's croak and a wren's song. Other noises,

242

though, scratched the back of her mind like unwanted thoughts, and the darker the forest got, the harder she listened for the familiar.

"What's out there?" she wondered aloud.

Calithan didn't respond at first but kept walking. Finally, as they rounded an immense oak tree, he said, "*A myriad of peculiar notions, virtuous in no way and abundant beyond measure.*"

And the world behind him blasted into a spectrum of exploding prisms and bass notes, of lights and sounds with no context. An unknown realm that Molly's mind tried its best to construct into something Molly could understand—could take in.

She fell to the ground holding her ears and tightly closed eyes. She jumped when Calithan touched her shoulder.

"*You can't stay here, Molly,*" he said, his voice sounding distant and fading fast. "*You've got to continue the walk.*"

Molly slowly opened her eyes. Somehow she was no longer in a dark forest but instead sitting at the base of an enormous mountain. A bundle of small gray rocks, disturbed from its place above by some unseen source, came rolling down fifty feet in front of where she sat. She didn't see Calithan, but there was a piece of paper folded in half in her hand that read:

From here, you go on without my escort, so I leave you with some advice. Keep in mind that this realm will distract you from your desires—from your dreams, your goals. Often with fear and intimidation but sometimes with unfathomable beauty and wondrous applause.

Do not give in.

Do not lose sight.

And, when you get where you are going, tell Story my debt is repaid and not to call on me in such a manner ever again.

C

Molly took in the cryptic message with a deep breath, crumpled up the note, and screamed in frustration.

Juniper

Juniper awoke with a start. She sat upright in her bed, her eyes puffy from crying, and listened to the quiet of her house. Molly wasn't yelling out another girl's name anymore. Juniper climbed out of bed—she hadn't remembered falling asleep—and wiped her nose on the sleeve of her hoodie. She returned to the window to see if she could see her grandma anywhere.

Everything seemed still and silent, yet energized. Like arriving at the theater after the players have left the stage and the audience has gone home.

Juniper began to pace. She picked up a mason jar from her desk, looked at the walking stick in it, and then put it back down, the walking stick seeming oblivious to her state of mind.

She walked over to her bedroom door and opened it a crack, straining to hear out into the rest of the house without actually having to leave the sanctuary of her room, but didn't hear anything. Nothing out there that would suggest her grandma, who Juniper worried might be sick, was waiting to grab her and confuse her some more.

Finally, Juniper opened the door entirely and stepped into the hallway.

There was no noise at first beyond the creaking of the floorboards with each step Juniper took. Then, a whirring sound, woosh-woosh-woosh, from down the hall, but that was the ceiling fan from Molly's room, Juniper knew. Slowly she made her way to the doorway.

"Maybe she's asleep," Juniper hoped, her heart pounding in her ears.

She hurried the last few steps down the hall and peeked around the doorway into Molly's room. Her grandma's bed was empty. Taking a quick look around, but only from the doorway, Juniper exhaled the breath she didn't realize she'd been holding and continued her way to the top of the stairs. She turned off the light as she left the room.

This is silly, she admonished herself inside her head. *I don't need to be afraid of my grandma.* Juniper took the first five steps carefully down the stairs "Grandma?" she asked aloud. Her voice fell into the house as though a whisper in an empty jar.

Molly wasn't home.

Lost By

Moonlight

Timberhaven

Tod enjoyed hurting people.

He didn't remember a time when that wasn't the case—when his body didn't buzz like he'd eaten an entire box of candy at the sound of someone crying out in anguish. True, things had amped up in the destruction and misery-dealing of late, but Tod wasn't self-aware enough to realize such things.

He was just enjoying the ride.

Tod *really* wanted to make Junkyard cry. Something about that brat bugged him. Always tooling around with some book or another, building this or that. Jake wouldn't shut up about the little witch.

No, Junkyard *needed* knocked down a peg or two, and Tod was just the man for the job. Hell, he'd already killed a kid for his guitar today. Tod was on top of the world.

Might as well make it two, he thought.

"Tod, it's the pigs!" Curtis whispered, snapping Tod out of his thoughts as the trio rode their bikes along the trail in the woods. The spinning red and blue lights on two police cruisers lit up the trees around the Steadherd residence.

Tod skidded to a halt, his lackeys pulling up on either side. The sheriff was talking into his radio in Tod's front yard, but he wasn't alone. Two EMTs were loading someone on a gurney into an ambulance—a man, by the sound of his screaming.

Tod couldn't help but smile.

"I'm out of here," Bobby said. He picked up his bike and spun it around, aiming to return the way they'd come, but Tod pushed him and his bike over.

"No," Tod said, staring at Bobby.

Bobby glared back.

"Um, guys," Curtis said, trying to break the tension. "Sheriff's on the move."

"Can't you give him something, for cripes' sake?" Sheriff Vindego asked the EMTs. "He's dying!"

The EMTs responded, but the boys couldn't hear their response.

"Fine, just get him to County General," the sheriff sighed. "You're gonna be okay, Ollie. They're going to take great care of you."

But Deputy Barnhart only screamed as they finished putting him into the ambulance and shut the doors.

"Look, Larry, I don't know," Sheriff Vindego returned to the radio. "His hand is gone, sheered off through the bone, and the rest . . . looks like a mountain lion got to him. No one else is at the Steadherd place, so I don't know what the hell. They're shooting Ollie up with something once he's loaded in the ambulance to quit the screaming, so I won't get anything out of him anytime soon. Look, don't mention this to anyone yet, not with what happened to Sherry's husband. I'm going to take another look around here. Over."

"*I'll keep on lid on things until you say otherwise. Careful, sheriff,*" Larry's voice came over the radio.

"Will do," Sheriff Vindego said. "Do me a favor, call over to Sugars. Don't say anything about what's gone on here tonight, but tell them I'll be stopping there later and to keep Denise handy. She has a world of trouble about to land on her head with this boy of hers. Over and out."

Tod slowly backed his bike down the trail, away from the flashing lights of the cop cars. Bobby got up, and he and Curtis followed their leader.

"He's going to tell your mom!" Curtis whispered.

Tod flicked Curtis' forehead.

"Wouldja shut up!" Tod hissed. "Not until we're out of earshot of the pig."

The trio got further into the woods as the sounds of the night enveloped their conversation.

"What do I care about him talking to my mom?" Tod asked. "Way I see it, that frees us up for more fun with Junkyard."

"How do you mean?" Curtis asked. "She's home with her grandma."

Bobby's eyes widened, and a smile was noticeable even in the dark. "We're finally going to hit her *and* her grandma?"

"Boys," Tod grinned, "the fun is *just* starting tonight."

The Pitch

Under a starless black sky, Veneswill walked to and fro across the muddy puddle on his padded mastodon feet, splishing and splashing like a child at play. But, while a baby's face adorned the end of his trunk, the inchlong Pitchborn was no child.

Veneswill was an emperor.

Though he didn't take much pride in the status.

That Veneswill was the wisest of the Pitchborn, the craftiest creature in this nightborn realm, was known. The bar for wisdom amongst most of his fellow citizens being what it was, however, meant that this was not what Veneswill would call an accomplishment.

The downside of being the smartest, Veneswill found, was that you didn't have anyone to take your problems to so you could sort them out.

And, though he was the tiniest Pitchborn, too, Veneswill had big problems.

The Emperor of Refuse watched as more of his subjects —a herd led by three fur-lined ribcages covered in snake-like tendrils and an inside-out pelican with mismatched feet— wandered up a rocky cliffside into the green mist at the edge of his realm, exiting his domain for parts unknown. He knew what it was that called the empty-headed creatures, summoning them toward the exits. Veneswill couldn't hear the call nor feel its pull, but the results on the rest of his kind were evident.

Claptrap needed to be found, or Veneswill would soon be the ruler of an empty kingdom.

Veneswill stepped before his Augment Glass, the machine the human had helped him build many years before. Veneswill hadn't known the toll that building the glass would take on the already weakened wall between The Pitch and the man's world (or the cost that the man would end up having paid), but he would doubtfully have done things any differently if he had.

Finishing the glass had resulted in consolidating his power, after all.

Veneswill powered up the Augment Glass, and a version of his inchlong body appeared before his people, now seven stories tall, towering over the herd of escaping Pitchborn. Veneswill waved his trunk about, the screaming baby face at its end railing back and forth over the crowd to get the attention of the simple-minded creatures.

First, only one or two Pitchborn, the ones with eyes, noticed, but soon, their fear spread throughout the herd, allowing Veneswill to swing his trunk and knock the creatures off their path of escape into another realm. Such was the power of the Augment Glass. It could make Veneswill appear big, but it also needed the other Pitchborn to *believe* he could hit them to complete the spell, making that fear a reality.

With the other Pitchborn dispatched from their dreamlike trance and moving away from the green mist again,

Veneswill stepped back from the Augment Glass and returned to his pacing.

It must *be Agares*, Veneswill regathered his train of thought. *He's the only other Pitchborn still living to exhibit any kind of control over our kind beyond The Ancients.* At this, Veneswill inadvertently gazed at the lone tower across from his dais of mud and gore. As Emperor, Veneswill felt it well within his right to demonstrate his power from atop a platform, but even he didn't dare to approach the height of the tower of The Ancients.

The smokeless green flame burned eternally as a promise of their return, and Veneswill would not tempt being the cause.

Returning to his pacing and thinking, Veneswill turned away from the tower. *The problem with condemning him to the Hollows of Nil, however, is that I cannot know if the stinking fiend has discovered a way to worm himself out of his prison!*

Veneswill reared back on his hind legs and brought his front legs smashing down again, the baby face on the end of his trunk screeching in a rage.

The tantrum ended, Veneswill looked toward the green mist once more. Agares' pet Pitchborn, lost in the realm called Timberhaven, was crucial to his plans, Veneswill knew. So, Claptrap must be removed from the board.

I need word from my inquisitors, he decided.

Timberhaven

Story doubled back a third time. Molly, or the body that belonged to Molly, at any rate, kept getting distracted, wandering off despite the brown tabby's protests.

"We're nearly there, Rodger," Story purred. "Just a little further."

Story didn't know the current whereabouts of Molly's spirit, but the cat understood that the sooner the pair were reunited, the better.

Discovering who was driving Molly's body hadn't been difficult to figure out once the yelling outside Juniper's house had started.

"I'm losing my mind," Rodger-in-Molly's body said. He watched as a car drove slowly past the odd couple—just an older woman out having a moonlit stroll with her cat—and couldn't place the model of the vehicle. "I'm talking to a cat telling me it knows where my daughter is."

"I said I could help," Story corrected him.

"Yes, well, regardless," Rodger reached out and grabbed a leaf from a tree at the sidewalk's edge. "And how is it I don't remember there being sweetgum trees along Landrum Street? Judging by their size, they had to have been planted twenty years ago at least!"

Story rubbed alongside and in between Rodger's legs, continuing to coax him along.

"Everything will make sense once we get to Kings Park," Story said.

Rodger took some staggered steps forward, still looking at the tree and shaking his, or rather, Molly's, head, but eventually, he followed the cat.

"I think maybe I'm dreaming," Rodger said, focusing on the brown tabby before him. "How else can I be conversing with a cat?"

"Yes," Story said. "I can understand how it would make sense to see things that way. I imagine it feels like you've been dreaming for a long time."

Rodger thought about that as they walked but didn't respond, so Story continued.

"Dreams are funny that way," Story said, guiding the pair around the corner and across the next street. They were closing in on The Pavilion then. Not much further to Kings Park. "Sometimes you can piece stories together that began somewhere else, long ago. If you've got the knack for it."

Rodger stopped. "Stories?"

Story turned back to face him. "The big picture. Dreams can help you fill in gaps that you might not realize are there, or maybe you've forgotten."

Molly's hands ran over her face, covering up a big inhale of breath, then exhaling it again. But it was Rodger who asked, "What have I forgotten?"

"Let us continue your dream," Story said, returning toward Kings Park. "And find out together."

Molly

Molly got up.

For some reason, she slid Calithan's crumpled note into the pocket of her dress (presuming then that this was a bizarre dream because her dress *had* pockets) and looked around.

"Mountains," Molly sighed. "Or *a* mountain anyway." She walked.

Eventually, the mountain path she was on began to change into a slight road that hugged the mountain's base. Every so often, Molly thought the gray rocks she kept seeing at the foot of the mountain would blink at her with some inherent light source, but she could never catch it happening well enough to persuade herself she wasn't imagining things.

Molly began to get lost in her thoughts, attempting to formulate any plan, but then she'd start thinking about Juniper. Then, back to coming up with any idea of how to get out of the state she'd found herself in, dream or not.

The clicking noise, Molly realized, had been matching her steps, hidden in her footfalls, but she didn't know for how long. She stopped a split-second before the sound, proving it was real.

You're smarter than this, Molly chided herself. *Acting like you didn't grow up in Timberhaven.*

Molly whistled a long, high note, then pitched it higher until trailing off.

Silence.

It's not a Ponder Bird, then, she figured. *Or it'd echo my call.*

Molly continued walking, leaving the road and willing her ears to pick up any sound in the rocky hills around the mountain. The distance looked filled with more hills and rocks, the mountain being the only distinguishable landmark.

Maybe some dream logic, then.

Molly sat down. She rested her arms on two round, gray stones, one on either side and stretched her legs out in front of her, opening herself up to her environment. It was windless in the surrounding hills, and the sky was mud-colored with no clouds. Everywhere smelled vaguely of dirt, of old. Forgotten.

This brought Molly back to songs. She didn't know why she felt that a song would make or break her fate, but Molly locked in on the idea. She focused as intensely as she could on songs she knew.

Come on, Molly closed her eyes. Right then was the most coherent she'd felt in ages. She would think of a song, begin humming it, then decide it didn't feel right in her mouth.

The Song of Summoning.

The Gypsy Moth Song.

The Vanilla Ice Cream At the Summer Swing Song

None of them were *the* song. Molly lay in the dirt, surrounded by gray rocks that sometimes may or may not glow, fighting the urge to cry. She'd shed too many tears of late and wouldn't do so now.

The clicking started again.

Molly sat upright and got to her feet. The sound was closer. Though, with three hundred and sixty degrees of unblocked scenery around her, its origin was still lost.

"Enough!" Molly shouted. "Come at me if you're coming!"

The clicking sound ramped up, with more than one source—first two, then another, several. Like cicadas in summer, Molly was overwhelmed by the sounds of clicking.

Then she saw what was coming for her.

Juniper

Juniper stopped at the bottom of the stairs. She checked that the front door was still locked, then peeked through the curtain onto the front porch. The streetlight bathed wicker chairs, potting soil, and the porch swing, but Juniper didn't see her grandma among them.

Juniper turned and walked into her grandma's living room, taking in the art and antiques that decorated the room. Some her grandma had done, like the painting of the black woman singing on top of a piano while a man played a trumpet in the background. Juniper had always liked that one.

"Grandma?" Juniper called again, a little louder this time. She continued walking into the kitchen, where she found a pot partially filled with water boiling over on the stovetop. Juniper turned off the burner and moved the pot. She sighed, shaking her head at the box of egg noodles, two cans of tuna, and a small basket of shelled sweet peas nearby. Handwritten recipes for various dishes were stuck by magnets to the refrigerator, taped to the inside cabinet doors, and sticking out of multiple cookbooks stacked around the kitchen. Still, it always came down to tuna casserole for her grandma.

Juniper grabbed a yellow apple and took a big bite, unable to remember exactly when she had eaten last. She peeked through the curtain of the back door, but things looked similar to the front: a nighttime filled with ambient street lights but no grandma. Juniper walked around and out of the kitchen toward the two extended bookshelves that stood as sentries along either side of the hallway that led back to the front door.

"First, Slow goes missing," Juniper said, running her fingers over the spines of her grandma's books as she ate her apple with her other hand. "Now I don't know where Jake is. And Grandma is acting funny." Juniper stopped at a book entitled *What Now?* and pulled it out far enough to check the cover. It was about steps to help you overcome grief, so Juniper pushed it back in.

"I need something about monsters . . ." Juniper told the empty room.

The crash came from the backyard, causing Juniper to crouch and look toward the window at the end of the hall. A long shadow, cast by the streetlight, crawled across the wooden fence that separated Juniper's grandma's yard from their neighbor's. Juniper dropped her apple and crawled to see who was there.

She stopped at the wall and slowly raised her head high enough to look out the window, letting out a quick scream.

Juniper was eye-to-eye with an intruder, separated only by a pane of glass.

She scurried backward and got to her feet, running toward the staircase upstairs, when she saw another shadowy silhouette standing at the front door, its features only cloudy through the lace curtain.

"She's headed your way, Curtis!" a voice rang out from the backyard just as the crash of broken glass came from the kitchen. Someone—Curtis, it would seem—began to pound on the front door and jerked its handle.

Another window exploded from the kitchen as Curtis confirmed Juniper's worst fears from the front door, peeking at her through a slight divide in the curtains.

"Juuuuunkyaaaaard," Curtis sang through gritted teeth. "We're heeeeere."

Unable to help it, Juniper screamed again and ran upstairs.

Slow

Slow continued playing the empty air, fingering his absent guitar, lost in his song. To his credit, Collin did not speak to Slow any further as the pair followed the green light stones rolling to freedom. Though Slow would occasionally catch the man mumbling something.

I hope this is a good idea, Slow thought, staring at his companion in the dim light.

As if reading his mind, Collin looked over and caught Slow looking. He smiled what Slow assumed Collin thought was a reassuring smile, but Slow was anything but reassured.

As Slow watched, though, Collin's eyes widened as his face was caught simultaneously in a second light source.

"Out," Collin spoke the word softly, as if he feared doing so would break the spell. "I'm finally out!"

Slow turned as the stones rolled out, exiting the caves and into the open air. His arthritic hands stopped their playing, but his feet picked up their pace.

"We made it," Slow said.

Collin stood with his back straight, his head tilted, staring into an open sky the color of mud. The small gray stones, their green light no longer pulsating, seemed to sway slightly at his feet like hunting dogs awaiting a command.

Slow, now an old man emulating his name, quickly felt the need to be rid of his walking companion.

"We're outside now, so," Slow began walking away, "I'll be going."

Collin spoke in a booming voice, words that Slow had never heard before, let alone understood. Collin raised his arms as his voice grew louder. Once pale and sickly, his skin began to take on a healthier hue, but his small, dark eyes stayed darker for the effort.

Then Slow heard clicking from somewhere in the distance, conjuring the image of hundreds of crabs walking across the tile of his mind.

"Oh, don't go," Collin said, still staring at the empty sky. "Not yet. Just wait one more moment."

A nightmare came over the hills then—scores of nightmares—as Slow watched. Hundreds of miscast creatures, ill-formed and misbegotten by inattentive gods, rushed toward the mountain's base.

Toward him.

Or, more to the point, toward Collin.

"Yes, my children," Collin's voice boomed, "I am returned."

Amidst the sea of gangly, molted fur-covered arms, legs, and necks, with the occasional reptilian skin or shimmering scale, Slow made out a woman in their company. She was bound, hurried like willful cattle, but she was human.

"What is—" Slow began, but Collin spun his head quickly toward Slow, shutting him up.

"Yours, Slow, was a song astray," Collin spoke so softly that Slow could hardly hear over the approaching horde. "But, having escaped my prison, I no longer need rudderless, forgotten." Collin's face beamed as the monsters surrounded him until, finally, his eyes fell on the woman in their captivity.

"I'll be penning the next arc in the story," Collin sneered. "*My* story. And this time, I need a song of anguish."

The woman pulled away, pushing back into the onslaught of creatures around her, but they shoved her back toward Collin. Slow thought then that he recognized her from somewhere.

"And yours, Molly, is exquisite," Collin continued, wetting his lips. "I've been able to listen through my minion. Your pain has been a salve, getting me through many a lonely night." The woman began to sob under the stare of Collin until she was wailing in misery. Her legs collapsed under her, but she was kept upright by the mob of monsters.

Slow tried to push into the crowd to get to the woman, but his arthritic hands folded into a fuzzy shoulder, costing him his balance. Slow hit the ground, and he felt his hip give out. A cough racked his lungs as he silently cursed his old body.

Then, the monsters fell upon him, gouging, kicking, and biting.

"No!" Slow heard Collin's voice echo across whatever name belonged to this drab, desolate domain. "This boy is not to be harmed. Thus speaketh the Lord!"

Slow was losing consciousness. He felt his body lifted by the horde and brought before Collin.

"Tsk, tsk," Collin shook his head while wiping the blood from Slow's face. "You deserve, well, a great deal better than a beating at any rate." He grabbed Slow's lower jaw, staring him in the eye. "For your aid, I grant you leave. But mark your time in your world well, boy. Enjoy your respite while you're able. For I will be coming not long behind, and I bring endings."

With that, Winslow Perkins, Slow to his friends, disappeared.

"Now," Collin said, grabbing the crying woman from his mob. He shoved a lop-sided bear; its fur was nearly all burnt off, and it had no face. "Let us away to the gate out of this wretched hole. I've my army of your brothers and sisters to gather before the storm, and this," Collin jerked Molly's face toward him, "is just the flavor of pain I need to unite them."

Timberhaven

Since becoming sheriff, Brock Vindego had collected more than a few wild stories: drunks falling from bridges and getting pulled from the lake completely unhurt, farmers calling in Squatch sightings, and the like. People'd listen to those tales, oohing and ahhing at the right spots, suspending their disbelief as needed because you never know. Things like that *could* happen. The Sheriff never shared stories that took place in Timberhaven, though.

No one would believe them.

Until the day he died, Sheriff Vindego never knew what made him stop by Molly Matheson's place on his way to Sugar's. It could have been police training running in the background of his mind. Tod Steadherd and his thugs had attacked Molly's grandaughter earlier that evening in the park, and her house was the last stop Deputy Barnhart had made before being ripped to shreds at the Steadherd home. You had to investigate. Get to the bottom of things, even if those things don't make sense, like his deputy lying in a hospital after being attacked by some kind of animal—the second such incident in one day—though there were no signs of any outside of the mangled bodies.

Sheriff Vindego, lost in thought on how he would approach Tod's mom, Denise, wasn't running his sirens or overheads during the drive over. There was no reason to. But as he pulled around, the beams of his cruiser's headlights crossed the Matheson place. The house was dark, but Brock saw a figure dart away from the front door and jump off the porch. He fired up his overheads and painted the scene in the familiar red and blue lights.

The sheriff parked his cruiser, stepped out, and yelled through the speaker.

"*This is the sheriff!*" his voice boomed back at him off the house and nearby trees. "*Come around to the front of the house, now! Don't make me come after you, Tod.*"

Brock couldn't swear that he'd seen Tod Steadherd on the porch, but he was hedging his bet that night, given the evening's events.

"Scatter," a voice came from behind the house. "It's the pigs!"

Sheriff Vindego ran around to the side of the Matheson home and immediately saw two figures, both young males, trying to scale the backyard wooden fence.

"Do not move!" he shouted, running into the yard to the corner of the house. So, not Tod, but he's cronies. Curtis Eubanks, the heavier set of the two, fell from the fence and hit the ground hard. However, the second of the pair—the sheriff couldn't remember. Bobby something—quickly made it over and began to run. The sheriff could see his head over the fence, heading toward the woods.

Sheriff Vindego made a gamble then, yelling into the darkness ahead for backup he did not have.

"He's headed right for you guys, Beaumont, Higgins. Light him up!"

The second boy stopped short and put his hands up just as the sheriff got to Curtis lying on the ground. He took out his handcuffs and helped the downed boy sit up.

"You're fine," the sheriff told him as Curtis tried to catch his breath. "You just got the wind knocked out. You," he pointed to the escapee, "get back over the fence and sit with your buddy."

Once the pair were seated together on the ground, Sheriff Vindego handcuffed them to each other through the fence.

"Where's your leader?" Sheriff Vindego asked, looking back to the Matheson house. The back door was hanging broken, and a side window had been shattered.

The house was still dark inside.

Juniper

Juniper heard the back door bust open just as she reached the second floor, turning off every light she could on her way. She jumped to grab the hanging cord suspended in the hallway, pulling the ladder to the attic down as quickly as possible, remembering what Jake had taught her earlier in the day: that as mean and hateful as his brother was, Tod wasn't hard to trick.

Juniper ran past as the ladder popped onto the floor, fully extended. She rounded the corner into her grandma's room, ducked behind a dresser, and waited, convinced that Tod would hear her panting for breath.

"Juuuuuunkyard," Tod's voice sang hoarsely from the dark. "We're not going to hurt you," he lied. "Well, maybe a little."

Tod began to climb up the ladder to the attic. "All the flavors of pain we'll get to introduce you to."

Juniper listened as her bully rambled, sounding like he wasn't even talking to her anymore, just talking. Tod's voice made her shiver as he walked around her grandma's house like he owned the place. She waited until she could hear his footsteps in the attic, then moved toward the window near her grandma's bedside. A trellis covered in flowering ivy ran down to the ground. All Juniper had to do was open the window quietly, and she'd escape.

Supposing Curtis and Bobby weren't waiting at the bottom.

The thought made Juniper freeze. She was still unmoving, even when she didn't immediately see them standing outside, when she heard Tod's voice from the attic again.

"The pain!" he yelled, smashing something.

Juniper could move once again. She placed her tiny fingers under the frame of the window and pulled. The window creaked but didn't budge. Juniper tilted her head, trying to make her ears work extra to hear if Tod had heard, but the bully's footsteps still trudged upstairs as though he had all the time in the world. No hurry. Taking a breath, Juniper looked up at the lock on the window, drawn closed. She shook her head, annoyed at herself, and unlocked it.

The window opened quickly after that.

Juniper's hoodie caught on the bottom of the window and bunched around her head as her little legs found purchase on the trellis, forcing her to hold up and rearrange her clothes. Once she was properly wearing her hoodie and was assured her Tesla coil was still safely inside, she stopped to listen. There was some kind of commotion on the other side of the house.

Juniper hurried down the trellis again, worried that the other boys had figured out her escape plan. Her hood caught on some of the ivy and pulled up, falling over her head. Undeterred, Juniper looked down at her feet and, one sure step after the other, found solid footing until she was on the ground.

Had she only taken her hood down, Juniper would have seen Sheriff Vindego's patrol car coming down her street. As it was, she hadn't and ran for the woods instead.

<u>Timberhaven</u>

From the attic window of Molly Matheson's house, Tod *had* seen the patrol car and quietly made his way for the window in Molly's room.

Because he'd seen how Juniper had escaped the house, too, as she headed into the woods, eluding him.

And that would not stand.

There would be no escaping the punishment she had coming to her again, not tonight.

Tod slid out the open window of Molly's room, down the trellis, and into the woods, stalking his prey and listening, uncaring, as the sheriff captured his friends behind him.

Slow

Slow awoke with a start, scaring the three women watching over him. He was on a couch in a small room, maybe an office. The smell of fall was wafting in upon a cool breeze through an open window. The woman who had a cool rag on his forehead felt his cheek.

"You're okay," the woman said, whispering comfortingly to Slow. "It's going to be all right."

"Who," Slow said, slowly moving his head back and forth, trying to reclaim the fifteen-year-old version of his body as his own. "Where am I?"

"I am called Essa," the woman said. She pointed to the other women in the room. "This is Nickie. She helped me keep your body well until Brynne," she pointed at a red-headed woman, "could help your spirit find it again. You were in my fountain."

It came back to Slow then, the bullies, going under the fountain's water, everything.

"Yvette!" Slow sat up straight, searching the room.

"There was no Yvette," Essa said.

"Is she your friend?" Nickie asked.

"No, no, no," Slow muttered, getting to his feet. "She's my most prized, my—" Slow sat back down on the couch, hard, dizzy from the effort.

"She's his guitar," Brynne said, sitting beside him.

"This was all that was left near you in the fountain," Essa said, holding up what looked like a small speaker.

"My Pignose," Slow sighed, taking it and holding it in his lap. "The amp for my guitar."

"Look, Essa," Nickie said. "The kid's clearly been robbed, nearly killed. It's time to call the Sheriff."

"No!" Slow said, a little louder than he'd intended. "There's, uh, no need. Besides, there's something more important." Slow began trying to push through the fog in his brain, remembering. "A woman, an old lady. Molly is her name, I think. Someone…something is going on. She needs help."

"It is as you saw, then," Essa said, looking at Brynne. "And as I feared. I must tell Gerald we'll be closing early this evening. Come, Nickie, let us leave her to work." Essa said, leading Nickie out into the hall.

Brynne smiled gently at Slow and took his hands in hers, closing her eyes.

"I think—" Slow began to stand.

"It's going to be all right," Brynne interrupted, sitting him down once more.

"What are you doing?" he asked. Brynne's hands felt warm in Slow's.

"You're safe." Brynne's eyes were still closed but fluttering under her eyelids as if she were reading quickly. "So, now I want to try to help Molly, and to do that, I need your help."

Slow sat silently as the woman moved her head back and forth as though trying to make out someone she knew in a moving crowd.

"Molly's spirit is…was, lost somewhere outside our world," Brynne said, her eyes still closed. "But now she's with someone. Some things. Oh, oh no!" She opened her eyes and stood. "I must warn the others. Kings Park!"

As the red-headed woman ran out of the room, her cryptic message lost on Slow, he made up his mind.

Well, good thing I already know where Kings Park is. Slow thought, gathering his things. *Thanks, kiddo.*

Leaving without saying thank you to the trio of women felt wrong, but Slow slid out the open window anyway.

Juniper

By the time Juniper heard the sheriff call out over the radio, it was too late to try and get back to him. Tod was already between her and safety.

Hearing the sheriff over the speaker had been lucky, Juniper thought, because now she at least knew that Tod was hot on her trail and not still wandering around her grandma's house, wrecking the place.

Juniper immediately changed course, trying her best not to make so much noise as she ran through the forest, though it was difficult to do in the dark. She'd get around one low-hanging branch or bush just to get entangled in another or trip on a rock or root, then slip in the mud.

I'm making too much noise, her mind kept telling her. *Tod's going to get me, and I don't know what to do.*

Tears began to well in Juniper's eyes, and she felt heavy breaths coming as her lower lip protruded, but she went on, losing track of how long she'd been zigging and zagging through the forest. At one point, Juniper thought there was a faint green light all around, hardly visible, but then things grew darker and darker between the trees, so she shrugged it off as her mind playing tricks.

The night and the trees and the bushes began to make Juniper feel like she was wandering in another world, some alien place. But then Tod would call out mockingly from the black, forcing her back to her situation.

"Junkyard. Juuuuunkyaaaard. I'm gonna get you!"

Sometimes, his voice sounded close, and Juniper would stop to listen, doing her best to be quiet. Then, Tod would call out again and sound further away, so Juniper would continue.

Finally, Juniper reached a clearing in the woods where the trees weren't so close, and she could see the sky. Only, there was no sky to see—no stars, no moon, no clouds—just that same faint green light, almost like pictures of auroras that Juniper had seen in books, but not as distinctive.

"The sky has gone funny, wouldn't you agree?" a familiar voice called out from in front of Juniper, making her jump.

It was Mr. Jack.

Juniper ran twenty feet toward where his voice had come from, bumping into Mr. Jack sitting on a rock and falling into him.

"Careful, now! You wouldn't want to—" but he left the thought unfinished when the little girl hugged him, crying. "Aww, there now. It's okay."

After a few minutes, having finally released her nerves a little bit, Juniper collected herself and stood up again, remembering the task at hand.

"We have to go, Mr. Jack," she said, wiping her eyes. "Tod is chasing me!"

Mr. Jack leaned back and picked up something beside the rock. In the dim green light, Juniper saw that it was a guitar.

"Slow's guitar!" she shouted, then caught herself, whispering, "Mr. Jack, that's Slow's. Which means," she looked around marking the scene. "I know where we are now."

"I wondered if it might be." Mr. Jack said, fiddling with the guitar. "I stumbled over it here a moment ago and saw that it had a string needing mending." Satisfied with his adjustment of Slow's broken guitar string, Mr. Jack stood and slid the guitar's strap over his shoulder, letting it sit on his back.

"Now we can head on." Mr. Jack smiled. "Your friend should be able to play admirably once again, after he tunes his instrument, of course. As to the matter of our young Jake," Mr. Jack's head sagged, "I'm afraid I have not, as of yet, been able to locate him."

"Mr. Jack," Juniper pleaded, her stomach falling at the mention of Jake missing. She whispered as she looked around. "We've got to get out of here. Tod is coming after me. He's out there in the woods, too. We need to go!"

"We must go indeed, Ms. Soot," Mr. Jack offered the crook of his arm, "but that ruffian is the least of our concerns. You see, there are far worse things in the forest this night. In shapes and styles not of our world's making. We must away from Kings Park before—"

And then the monsters were upon them.

Slow

Slow crept back toward the rear of The Pub, away from the crowd of twenty-somethings exiting the front who were grumbling and mumbling about having to cut their night short. He froze for a beat when he saw the familiar fountain, his stage from earlier and also where he had nearly died. *Had* died, maybe. Slow would be the first to admit that he didn't fully understand anything that had happened to him since his arrival in Timberhaven, but he still felt something pulling—on his music, his memories, and pulling him toward the trouble in Kings Park.

Slow gripped his Pignose amp tight, the only thing he had on hand to use as a weapon, and headed into the park.

A mist was coming from the park, billowing out of the trees around it in varying layers of deepening green. The streets were empty, and the sound of voices from The Pub grew quieter as Slow walked, nearly gone once the Kings Park sign was visible. Slow kept his head on a swivel and his arm loose, ready to swing. He wasn't about to get jumped by anyone or anything else tonight.

There was a figure there, in the fog. It was only a silhouette at first, until Slow walked closer and the shape began to form. It was a woman talking to a cat, but not any woman. He'd seen her twice before.

Molly.

Slow could hear her talking as he approached her, ten yards away.

"I think maybe I'm dreaming. How else can I be conversing with a cat?" Molly's voice echoed a bit, not unlike the first time Slow met her, if you could call what they'd done meeting.

"Ma'am?" Slow said, lowering his Pignose as he got closer. "Molly? My name is Slow, Winslow Perkins."

The green fog was getting denser between them.

"Stories?" she said, though she wasn't looking at Slow when she replied. She seemed very confused, lost.

"No ma'am," Slow said, hitching his Pignose to his belt as he continued toward her. "Slow."

She looked very sad then, looking down at the cat. "What have I forgotten?"

Slow was ten feet away from her. "Ma'am, I'm just going to help you. Some people are back at the bar, and well, they're looking for you. They'd like to help, too."

The woman and the cat turned away and continued into the green fog. Once she wasn't facing him, Slow couldn't hear what Molly was saying, so he picked up his pace to catch her as the green got more and more dense around them.

Then, she and the cat disappeared right before Slow's eyes.

The Pitch

Veneswill tried very hard to maintain his composure as he focused his thoughts across dimensions, but his patience was thin. The baby's face at the end of his trunk wailed, betraying his true emotions, as he continued pacing, only occasionally stomping his padded feet. To human eyes, the entire scene would have played out like a mouse throwing a conniption but trying to hide it.

"It almost went according to plan, Your Majesty," Whisper's thoughts came weakly across and into Veneswill's mind. "We've captured the Pitchborn but have suffered greatly for the effort."

Veneswill pushed a touch harder into his lackey's mind, taking in the scene through the small dog's eyes. Claptrap, the Pitchborn quarry that Veneswill had sent his minions after, was surrounded on three sides, bound by the Custom Triumvirate, a spell of Veneswill's own making. Of his captors, neither of the two dogs that Veneswill could see were unmaimed. The large one, Shadow, was missing a front leg. The mid-sized Row had a series of claw marks across his head. Claptrap had seemingly taken his left ear and eye.

"Why are you elevated?" Veneswill asked their leader.

At first, his question was met only with silence. Until finally, Whisper answered.

"I have lost the use of my legs," the pain in Whisper's mental response was evident. "The youngling, the boy who was our bait to lure the Pitchborn, carries me. I submit to this outrage, this embarrassment, only to see your will met. My lord."

"Enough complaining," Veneswill snapped. "Just get Claptrap through the gate and back to me."

"As you command," Whisper replied.

Veneswill sensed the small dog's anger as he responded, a slight growl growing in his belly, but the emperor was not bothered and ended their connection.

"Soon," Veneswill said, turning an about-face and pacing back the other direction. He glanced at the lines of Pitchborn forming, mindlessly bound away from his empire by some silent song, and powered up his Augment Glass once again.

"Soon, I'll have that cursed Pitchborn back, and Agares will lose everything."

Jake

Jake held the small dog close, mindful of her useless legs. His t-shirt was covered in blood, though none of it was his own. The monster had ripped into the pack of dogs fighting to get to him; Jake was sure of it. Now it was quiet, trudging along in the middle of their group like a zombie.

The thought made Jake shiver.

Whisper, whose eyes had been small slits, snapped to life.

"Mindful of your side, Row," she barked.

"I'm doin' my job, don't you worry," Row sulked.

"Not long now," Shadow bowed his head toward their small leader as he maintained his spot around the Pitchborn. "Just through the next bit of forest."

Jake thought that the large dog sounded sad. He looked down at the small dog in his arms and held Whisper gently as she shivered.

"How come I can hear you talk?" Jake asked, his curiosity momentarily trumping any fear born of the surreal night.

When Whisper didn't respond, angrily or otherwise, Shadow spoke up.

"See the green glow just above the tree line?" Shadow nudged his snout ahead. "Over there. And up above, too. All around the park."

Jake saw it then, disbelieving that he hadn't caught it before. A faint light emanated from the forest in and all around Kings Park.

"Whoa!" Jake gave a little boy's response. "Cool!"

"That's why you understand us," Shadow said. "And us, you."

"How long will this last?" Jake asked, his eyes wide with wonder. The fear he felt tamped down even further at the magic light that lets you talk to dogs.

"Shuddap before I eat you!" Row snarled, growling at Jake. Claptrap did a sort of stagger step.

"Stay in your place, mutt," Shadow growled in return. "I'll take your other eye if we lose our prize."

"Yeah, I'd like to see you try, Three-Leg," Row scoffed, but he tightened up their formation. Claptrap returned to his mindless shuffle.

"Best leave off talking until we're through the gate," Shadow spoke softly to Jake.

Jake looked through the trees and saw that Kings Park was now empty of people, not counting himself. A slight fog danced around the chess topiary—or fancy bushes, as Jake called them—tinged in the green glow of whatever magic spell the park was under. Between that and the moonlight, Jake saw shadows moving everywhere.

Then he saw some actual movement.

"Juniper?" Jake spoke his friend's name aloud, hopefully.

But it wasn't Juniper.

It was her grandma, walking with and talking to Juniper's cat. Suddenly, Slow was coming up behind them.

"Slow!" Jake yelled.

Slow didn't respond to Jake, but he was talking to Juniper's grandma.

"Silence!" Whisper commanded weakly. Row growled at Jake, causing Shadow to growl at Row, but both quieted after Claptrap shifted hard, trying to break free from their spell, and returned their focus to the job at hand.

"Not another word," Whisper told Jake once they had the Pitchborn steady again. She closed her eyes once more.

"But why don't they answer?" Jake asked. He watched in horror as Juniper's grandma disappeared into the green fog, followed seconds later by Slow.

"What happened?" Jake screamed. "Where did they go?"

Whisper awoke, finding enough strength to nip at the boy. Claptrap didn't make another escape attempt.

"Get us through," Whisper said, weaker still. "I will not leave a job unfulfilled. Let us be done with this." She then focused her eyes on Shadow and Row. "I do not want to die over there. Swear, if I do, you'll bring me back."

Both bigger dogs swore they would do as their leader asked. Whisper closed her eyes again.

"But, where are my friends?" Jake repeated, tears in his voice.

"They've entered the gate," Shadow answered in a low voice. "They've entered The Pitch. As are we."

The strange party of three dogs, a monster, and a little boy disappeared into the green.

Parade of

Pain

Juniper

The forest came alive in flashes of movement from the dark, taking Juniper and Mr. Jack amidst a sea of grunts, growls, and bruises. For his part, Mr. Jack went down swinging, attacking the night as best he could while unable to make out just what it was that was attacking them. Juniper ducked out of one grasp from furry, taloned paws only to be tripped up by a feathered wing or slimy leg.

Within minutes, the pair properly captured, the monstrous mob force-marched them deeper into the forest. Juniper still couldn't tell what had captured them, but whatever it was felt monstrous in the dark.

Like Jake's monster, Juniper thought. *Monsters are in New Town.*

Juniper desperately wished she knew where Story was.

"Listen, kiddo," It was Mr. Jack's voice from somewhere in front of Juniper, but he sounded weird. "I dropped the guitar in the ruckus, but it's gonna be okay. You got me? Just let me do the talking."

"You know what's happening?" Juniper asked. An antler of some kind jabbed her in the back, pushing her forward and making her cry out.

"Don't you touch her!" Mr. Jack yelled, shoving back in her direction through the crowd of creatures but failing to reach her. "Oof!"

"Mr. Jack!" Juniper shouted.

"It's okay, kiddo," Mr. Jack said, but he didn't sound okay to Juniper. "I'm not...I don't know exactly how I know, but this feels familiar. Like I've done it before."

"You're talking different," Juniper said. She kicked something soft as they walked and quickly bent to pick it up. It was Mr. Jack's hat. Juniper put it in her hoodie.

"Yeah," Mr. Jack said. "Things are different all over. But it's going to be okay."

They walked the rest of what felt like hours in silence, but eventually, the trees and bushes slid away into a rocky, muddy, open space. A large, green fire shone brightly from a tower in the distance, lighting everything in stark emerald and finally allowing Juniper to see their captors.

Her breath caught in her throat as she took them all in, the nonsense animals with their extra arms and legs, their wings that grew from nowhere. Some fur looked like moss, and some resembled dirty blankets. Then there were the misshapen people parts—eyes with teeth growing out of armpits and tongues with eyelashes coming from extra noses—all slapped together and tumbling along on spare body parts they had.

Monsters.

Their captors herded them away from the tower and toward a smaller dais when suddenly, a giant furry elephant towered above them.

"What is this?" The elephant—Juniper was stuck trying to remember what you called a furry elephant—mastodon or

309

mammoth—knowing that it had something to do with tusk sizes and teeth, when she noticed its trunk looked like a giant earthworm with a baby's head and face crying on it, causing her to scream—bellowed. "These are not the keepers of Claptrap!"

As they approached closer to the dais, Mr. Jack made a break toward it, bullrushing the creatures between them.

"I may not remember much about this place, but I remember how this works!" Mr. Jack yelled, diving onto the dais.

As he hit the platform, Juniper could make out a small, shiny purple reflection, a flash of some kind, just as the fuzzy elephant with the baby face trunk disappeared before them, replaced by a gigantic Mr. Jack.

"Run, kiddo!" The behemoth that was Mr. Jack yelled as he swung his enormous arms and hands at and through the monsters all around her. Whatever his plan, it seemed to have no effect, and the creatures surrounded him once again,

dragging him away.

The Pitch

Veneswill appeared once more in giant form, towering over the scene, his baby face laughing maniacally.

"Fool! You truly must not remember the powers of the Augment Glass. You may well grow to my magnificent size while standing before it, but my Pitchborn don't recognize you as a threat. They don't believe you can hurt them, so you can't, even at such a mighty height as this!"

Veneswill swung his trunk as if to demonstrate, flinging Pitchborn left and right in his glee.

Mr. Jack stood again, his face and neck bleeding.

"I was led to believe you were no longer alive," Veneswill said from his giant form, catching his breath from his tantrum. "Bring him to me," he barked at the Pitchborn closest to Mr. Jack. "The young human, too."

The giant form of Veneswill disappeared from the green-lit sky.

The Pitchborn surrounded Juniper and shoved her toward the dais as those around Mr. Jack did the same to him. As they got closer, Juniper saw that the purple flash she'd caught a glimpse of was a gem about the size of a can of soda and that the baby face-swinging fuzzy elephant was actually the height of a grasshopper standing on its hind legs.

Even in the face of the fear Juniper felt, and make no mistake, Juniper was very afraid, the scientist in her was taking in everything about the scene before her, dissecting things and trying to provide context for how this bizarre world worked. As for the Pitchborn, Juniper had to set them aside for the time being as their existence was too hard to make any sense of in light of her fear.

But the way that the purple gem, the Augment Glass, worked was coming together in her mind. As she worked it out, Mr. Jack's body dropped into the mud at her feet, and both he and she were pushed into the base of the dais as Pitchborn stood guard around them.

"It's a no-go," Mr. Jack said, seeming to read Juniper's thoughts. He sat up on his elbows, breathing hard. "You saw how it went. Even if I get big, I can't affect these things. They're like cattle," he said, spitting some blood. "But even more mindless. How do you make something like that afraid?"

How do you make them believe? Juniper wondered.

"Oh, now what?" Veneswill's tiny form screeched.

A new commotion erupted at the edge of the rocky terrain, coming out of the forest near where Juniper and Mr. Jack had arrived. A swath of Pitchborn tussled with something or someone while some of their brethren stood by, seeming confused about the situation. A few Pitchborn even began attacking their own.

Veneswill stood before the Augment Glass once again, his humongous form swinging his malformed trunk at the accosting Pitchborn and breaking things up. Once the scuffle cleared, Juniper could see who was at its center.

Tod Steadherd.

Her bully was bloodied, to be sure, his clothes tattered. But some of the Pitchborn circled him protectively, even going so far as to swipe at Veneswill as his mighty trunk swung by.

Veneswill's gigantic form reared, then brought both front legs down hard, smashing the stones around them as they hit and sending the nearby Pitchborn tumbling.

"What is this now?" Veneswill bellowed. "Oh, ho, ho. Agares is very clever. So you were who he's been calling to for aid. A human welp to help him out of his cage."

Tod kicked a Pitchborn who had fallen after Veneswill's outburst—a feathered otter with human knees for ears—as a few other Pitchborn began to rally around the human bully.

Such was the look on Tod's face that Juniper, who had been the victim of Tod's bullying many times, didn't recognize its rage and hate.

"Agares has strummed your strings too hard, it seems," the baby face on Veneswill's trunk giggled. "But still, I can't have his taint on you influencing my flock."

"Whose flock?" Juniper heard a voice boom from somewhere in the distance.

"I-impossible," Veneswill said, his mighty trunk dropping to the muddy ground.

They came then. A massive force of Pitchborn, nearly double the size of what swarmed around Veneswill. Pitchborn of all types—flyers, crawlers, runners, and diggers—swarmed toward the dais. And at their front walked a lone figure in a billowy white shirt and dirty pants.

A man.

And next to him, pushed and prodded by Pitchborn, a ghost of some kind. A woman's ghost.

"Grandma?" Juniper cried out.

Slow

Slow had a strong sense of deja vu once the green fog began to thin, and he could take in his surroundings. The starless sky, the silence of the forest. It was just like the beginning of this crazy, nightmarish adventure he'd found himself on since being drowned in the fountain outside of The Pub.

Only this time, he didn't have to walk the nightmare alone.

"Molly?" he asked the confused elderly woman he saw stumbling around some ten feet in front of him.

The woman looked up, evidently able to hear him now that the green fog had dissipated into the sky above.

"No," the woman said. "Not Molly. But, I get why you'd say so, given that this is her body."

"Ma'am?" Slow said, closing the gap between them slowly and carefully.

"The cat explained some," the woman said, holding out her hand. "Wherever it went. But I still don't really get it. Name's Rodger and this is my dream we're in."

"Believe it or not," Slow said, shaking her extended hand, "that's not the craziest thing I've heard today. I'm Winslow, but you can call me Slow."

"Well, I'll tell ya, it's been pretty wild, Slow," Rodger said. "I was making my kid dinner, and then the next thing I knew, I was walking around town in a woman's body with a talking cat. And it's the future, I guess? I dunno. Weirdest dream. I'm not much of a drinker, lucky if I ever finish half a beer, but I'm beginning to wonder if I overdid it before bed tonight. Anyhow, Ashley's never gonna believe this if I remember any of it in the morning."

Slow nodded. He didn't really know what to say.

"So, the cat said to walk this way," Rodger pointed with Molly's finger into the dark. "And that I'll remember what I've forgotten."

"I'm cool with that," Slow said, and the pair began to walk.

"How do you factor into my dream?" Rodger asked. "A talking cat, a kid in the woods, something I forgot. None of this tracks."

"Dream logic, I guess?" Slow offered. "I mean, I keep bumping into you—well, Molly—and I've never met her in real life. But dreams will do that, make a sense that's all their own."

Rodger mulled that over for a bit as they walked when, all of a sudden, she tripped on something, catching Slow's arm to keep her from falling.

"The hell?" Rodger said, looking down with an accusing glare.

"Yvette!" Slow yelled, bending to snag his best friend and favorite possession.

"What's a guitar doing in the middle of the woods?" Rodger asked. "Lemme guess, dream logic."

Slow looked Yvette over, clocking the nicks and scrapes, and gently strummed her as tears welled in his eyes.

She was home.

The Pitch

Agares held up his hands once he and his army were within less than a hundred feet of Veneswill's dais, and their forward march halted. The giant form of Veneswill reared back as a booming roar escaped from the baby's face on his trunk. The Pitchborn around the dais shifted slightly, feeling the tug of influence between two masters.

Juniper noticed as Tod, wild-eyed and panting through guttural grunts, shoved through a trio of bald chimps, whose ear lobes dangled to the ground in knots of slimy tentacles. Her bully stormed toward this new man and the ghost who looked like her grandma. Juniper's lower lip quivered at the sight of her.

"Ah, yes. My puppet," Agares smiled. "You couldn't get the job done, though, could you." Agares rolled up the sleeves of his tattered white dress shirt as Tod kept coming. "But no matter, no matter. As always, I solved the problem myself. Using another one of your failed conquests, might I add."

The Pitchborn parted ways as Tod sprinted toward Agares, his fists raised and his head forward, charging toward his intended victim like a mad boar.

As the boy got within five feet of him, Agares' voice roared, "SIT. DOWN."

And Tod stopped short, all energy expelled immediately as his legs gave out, dropping him to his knees.

Veneswill took the opportunity to attempt an attack, screaming at his army of mismatched creatures, "Take out this interloper! Now, kill him!"

The few Pitchborn who did move in for the kill were promptly either swayed to Agares' side or eaten by their brothers and sisters.

Veneswill reared again, bringing his gigantic front legs down on Agares, but his feet went straight through the man without effect.

Agares laughed, and as he did, the field of mud and stone echoed with the grunts, whinnies, and shrieks of his Pitchborn. Agares closed the distance between him and Veneswill within seconds.

"Trust me when I say this," Agares sneered. "I don't believe you can hurt me. And thus, there's not a Pitchborn on this field who believes it either." He leaned down and flicked the miniature Pitchborn with his index finger, flinging Veneswill into the stone behind the dais.

The sky above them was empty once again of threat.

Agares yelled in celebration, followed by the eruptive chorus of every Pitchborn behind him. He looked at the worn and weary pair of humans at his feet and crouched down to them.

"My, my, that felt good," Agares said. "Now, on to the task at hand." He grabbed Juniper by her hoodie and stood so quickly she didn't have time to scream.

Mr. Jack grabbed Agares around the legs, attempting to tackle them both to the ground. "Let her go!"

But Agares simply stood, holding Juniper up into the air with one arm while keeping Mr. Jack back by the scruff of his neck with the other.

"Ah-ah," Agares laughed. "I see your rage hasn't diminished, Rodger. But where is your pain? That exquisite agony you positively reek of is what I need currently. Come, come, Rodger."

"His name is Mr. Jack," Juniper said. She tried to aim her foot at Agares' face but was finding it difficult as she began to slide out of her oversized hoodie. She finally landed one strong kick right in Agares' throat.

Agares threw the child onto the dais, snarling, and pinned her to it, all while holding Mr. Jack's head against the front of the stone stage.

"I know who he is," Agares spat.

"Hey, let her go!" a voice rang out. Juniper's heart leaped, and she couldn't help but smile.

"Slow!" she yelled, looking his way. But then she froze because things didn't make sense. Slow was walking toward them all, but not alone.

Molly was with him.

Agares' eyes briefly went wide, but he covered before anyone noticed.

"Let her go, Collin," Slow demanded, walking a few quickened steps ahead of his companion toward the dais.

"We can let all pretense cease now, my young friend," Agares turned toward Slow, releasing Juniper and Mr. Jack. He raised both of his arms, showing his hands empty. "I am Agares."

"Fine, Agares. You say that like it should mean something. Okay, Juniper, come on," Slow said, waving the little girl to him.

Molly's body dropped behind him.

"Rodger?" Slow said, looking back.

"Oh, ho, ho, this is delicious!" Agares yelled. "Winslow, you've helped me even more than I could have dreamed!"

Juniper screamed as the *ghost* of her grandma fled toward the *body* of her grandma at the exact moment that a ghost of Mr. Jack *left* her grandma's body and *entered* Mr. Jack.

Slow turned back toward Agares to see that he had brought his hands down and crossed them before his chest. He began chanting in a low dirge, a bass note reverberating across the rocky terrain around them. The Pitchborn started to match the tone of Agares, amplifying things as Slow's Pignose did for Yvette, and the dirge became deafening.

Slow held his hands over his ears, just as Juniper and Mr. Jack did. Molly began to stir where she lay but quickly covered her ears as well.

"Pain!" Agares sang between chanting. "So much wondrous pain to paint with!"

Agares picked up the Augment Glass and held it aloft, continuing his dirge. Unbelievably, his Pitchborn army grew even louder—their belief in their master absolute.

Streams of purple energy began to beam out of the Augment Glass, finding purchase within each of Agares' chosen victims. One stream each plugged into Juniper, Rodger/Mr. Jack and Molly from within the confines of the gem.

In unison, they screamed in agony, some of their most painful memories broadcast across the sky like perverse home movies.

*   *   *   *   *

It was the middle of the night, and Rodger stood in Kings Park, ready to make yet another excursion into The Pitch to look for his beloved Melinda.

*"**You've got to stop this**," a man dressed in a brown suit with tails said, standing before the gateway. "**Your child***

fell to Claptrap as a means for the Pitchborn to anchor itself in Timberhaven," Calithan spoke without remorse. "I can offer you a semblance of revenge given time, but you've got to stop this. You were warned repeatedly—by me, Nicoline, the Council. The barrier is too fragile. It can't withstand your exploiting its cracks."

"Calithan," Rodger said, determined. "Get out of my way."

"Well, then, you leave me no choice," Calithan said. In a flash, he was upon Rodger, his hand covering Rodger's face as the devoted father screamed, his entire head awash in a brilliant, white light.

"I'll try to keep what I can of you," Calithan said with no emotion. "Jettison only the pain—bury the rage. But splaying is an imprecise practice, not as surgical as one might like. You will be different, just know. Altered. Still, you brought this on yourself."

Rodger fell to his knees, his thoughts on Melinda. Missing Melinda. She was his whole heart. Was she dead? No, not his daughter. Not Melinda. She had been a princess—his princess— trick-or-treating with her little orange Jack-o'-lantern. He had to save her. Save...her. Someone. Someone needed...saving? Savings? Better savings at $hop & $ave! Get your Jack-o'-lanterns, mister! Your Jack-o'—Jack. Mister.

Mr. Jack. That was his name. Right? What on Earth was he doing outside? And so late! It was preposterous, is what it was.

Mr. Jack found himself alone in Kings Park, which would become his home for many years, for better or worse.

The pain that had been his—had been Rodger's—floated away above him.

*   *   *   *   *

It began with a phone call, as these things sometimes do. Molly felt a pit in her stomach upon the first ring. She slowly got up from the table and measured each step to the phone with the increasing heaviness of her heart.

"Hello?" Molly whispered into the phone. She cleared her throat, speaking at normal volume. "Y-yes, this is she."

We're so sorry, ma'am. There's been a car accident. Your young daughter and son-in-law did not survive. They died quickly if that's any comfort.

Molly let out a sob. Not the type of sob that comes from heavy crying, those would come later and remain. It was the sound of the soul in anguish. When something deep inside cries out its pain, and the person who made the sound is left wondering how they will ever be capable of living in this world without the people they've lost.

Molly didn't know—couldn't have known—that a similar pain, one that had remained untethered for nearly fifteen years, was bound within the limits of Timberhaven. It flitted here and there, bouncing around its boundaries and *waiting for someplace to land. Energies so much alike and drawn to each other in cosmic coordinance.*

As Molly hung up the phone, Rodger's pain crashed into her head, tethering to her soul and rehomed in her brokenness.

By the time Molly came to any semblance of herself in those early days of their symbiotic shared living space, Rodger's pain gave her just enough space to learn that Juniper, her only granddaughter, had been living with Molly's son-in-law's people. Juniper, the last surviving part of the magic that was her daughter, Alice, might be happier where she was.

Molly wasn't any good to anyone, crying as she did all the time.

* * * * *

Juniper listened through the floorboards of her upstairs bedroom—a den, really. Transformed into a makeshift bedroom upon Juniper's arrival—her aunt and uncle talked below.

"Look, I'm not saying she's not a great kid. She is!" Juniper's uncle said.

"No, exactly. She's a great kid," Juniper's aunt agreed.

"It's just, we don't really have the room. I gave up my den—"

"Well, I couldn't give up my craft space," Juniper's aunt interrupted. "I've got two shows this year!"

"I know, I know," Juniper's uncle quickly interjected before his wife got going. "But that's my point. We're too busy for her right now."

And so it went as Juniper continued listening, lying on the floor of her uncle's den with tears in her eyes.

She missed her mom and dad. The music they made. They loved that their little girl was fascinated by science. Juniper loved the home they shared, just the three of them, and that it was gone made her heart hurt. She tried to hum the song her mom used to hum to Juniper at bedtime, but the tears began falling.

Then, Juniper was in Timberhaven, living with her grandma. But Molly only made tuna casserole and told her to stay safe. Stay out of the way.

Was there no one who wanted her now that her parents were gone?

Then came the day she found Tod and his friends in the woods. They had a dog pinned up in a makeshift kennel of dead wood and old fence.

And they were dousing the dog in gasoline.

The vision flashed forward a bit. Juniper was lying on the ground with a bloody lip and a torn shirt. Since she had somehow helped the dog to escape, the boys had made Juniper eat dirt before and after beating her.

"If you tell anyone about this," Tod said, his face beside hers. "We'll kill you. Not just you, though. We'll kill your grandma first. And that means anyone, ya hear me, Junkyard? Tell a soul, and we'll snatch yours right up!"

The bully needn't have bothered with his threats.

Juniper didn't have anyone to tell.

She was all alone in the world.

Molly

Molly's body was a burning nerve of electric ache, sharp and jagged, and yet somewhere, Juniper was screaming, causing Molly to open her eyes and find her grandbaby.

Though the pain was unbearable, Molly crawled toward Juniper, who was atop the dais. The purple energy stream attacking Molly's psyche, her very soul, had another tendril stretching from the stone Argares held and into her granddaughter.

As Molly writhed in pain in The Pitch's mud and loose stones, she had one thought, and it was entirely hers for the first time in longer than she could remember.

I can save her.

The deep chants of Agares' dirge brought out all the pain and sadness Molly had ever felt right to the surface of her mind, yet still, she crawled toward Juniper. The volume of the death song crept higher, but Molly kept on toward her grandchild.

Agares didn't notice what Molly was doing at first, preoccupied with his ecstasy as he was. By the time he did, Molly was already in place.

"Get away from there," Agares said, walking toward where she lay.

Molly sat up just enough to reach a hand into the stream of energy attached to Juniper, severing the connection to the child. Juniper's face went slack as she lost consciousness.

Molly, for her part, fell over in a fetal position as the pain she felt redoubled with two streams from the Augment Glass now flowing into her.

You won't survive this, Rodger's voice came into her mind. A welcome, if momentary, distraction from Molly's oncoming death. She wondered if it was because they'd effectively taken turns driving her body for so long, some kind of energy loop from the two of them both being connected to the Augment Glass, or if she was making up the sound of his voice entirely by telling herself something she already knew.

Maybe not, she told Rodger's voice, *but now Juniper might.*

Molly began to fade, losing herself, the strands of her life, piece by piece to the onslaught of Agares' attack. She watched as Juniper's misery show disappeared from the sky, leaving only hers and Rodger's. Wasn't that his name? And why was that woman up in the sky there crying? Who was on the phone?

Molly began to ponder such things less and less as her mind began to quiet, a sweet release from so much pain.

Slow

"Agares, stop!" Slow yelled, but it was no use. He could hardly hear his own voice over the sound of the collected army of Pitchborn intoning the death song. The pain in Slow's ears was overwhelming, but he tried to rush toward the man he'd brought out of the tunnels.

A swarm of discarded, sewn-together body parts—some human, some not—blocked his way from their master.

"I already gave you your out, Winslow," Agares' voice sounded like thunder over the noise. "Now, bear witness. There's nothing you can do to stop me. Just sit to the side and let this happen."

Slow felt the heat rise from his belly, the taste of copper in his mouth as his adrenalin spiked. He did not like this man, Collin, Agares—whatever his name was—acting like they were partners. Slow hadn't meant to release this monster from his cage, but he'd by God, do something to make that mistake right.

Slow raised his Pignose and began formulating an attack plan, patting Yvette hanging behind him to ensure his guitar was okay, and that's when it hit him.

This chanting had to go. It was time for some real music.

His.

Slow hung the Pignose on his belt and spun Yvette around, plugging her into the amp. The first chord was so quiet Slow could almost mistake it for being part of the noise. He turned the Pignose up all the way and played the chord again.

The Pitchborn around him shuddered as if cold.

Slow tuned his guitar a little and then strummed again.

The riff echoed over the field. Still outmatched by the chorus of chanting and the screaming of his friends, but the chord *was* there.

"What are you—" Agares' voice boomed. His approach to Molly interrupted by Slow's playing.

Slow began to play like he'd never played before, playing as though his life depended on it. Not just his but people he'd grown to care about, too. The monsters around him staggered back a little against his playing.

"Stop him!" Agares yelled.

Slow ducked behind a boulder but kept playing. He played blues, jazz, country, every song he could think of. Pitchborn crept around the corners of each side of his hiding spot, causing him to climb on top of the boulder, but still Slow played—bluegrass, followed by some hill music tunes he'd just picked up. Slow could tell his playing was beginning to overpower the guttural chanting, but it wasn't enough.

"Kill him," Agares ordered. This time, Slow could see the man from the tunnels barking orders and who he was talking to.

Tod stood up and began to run toward Slow.

This might be it, Slow thought, swallowing hard. *If so, I'm going out as me.*

He began to play *his* song. His soul as music. He played

as hard as he could, the Pignose vibrating against his thigh,

against a sea of monsters in a world backlit in forgotten.

Slow played.

Jake

"Was that," Row growled, seeing Juniper's giant memory playing across the sky through his one good eye. "Shadow, what were those whelps doing to Chance? We know that dog! He's a good boy!"

An intense anger roared up from Shadow's belly then, and Jake shuddered, though he tried not to wake the small dog he was holding.

"Be careful," Jake spoke quietly. "The monster is—"

But Claptrap took advantage of their distraction, breaking free from the spell that held him. He bowled into and over Row, biting and slashing as the pair tumbled, but quickly disengaged and ran for his brethren in the distance.

Claptrap was home.

Row coughed, getting up. "Lousy lowborn came at me from my blind side."

Shadow howled as the dirge from the Pitchborn grew louder.

"We must recapture him," the mastiff spoke through snarling teeth as his eyes darted, scanning the field of monsters in front of them.

Jake could feel the tears behind his eyes as he watched Juniper being sad on the sky TV. His fears had begun to creep back up at the sound of the scary singing and so many monsters in the dark place they'd found themselves in, but seeing Juniper sad and scared wrecked him, and he began to cry.

Then Jake heard guitar music. Quietly, at first. So quiet that he didn't trust his ears. But then louder. And the monster's chanting grew weaker in comparison.

"Slow?" Jake looked around to see where the music was coming from.

"There's one of Chance's attackers!" Row barked, and the pointer bound for the fray of monsters and music. Jake's eyes almost popped out of his head when he saw his brother.

"Row, stop!" Shadow growled.

"Leave him," a pitiful voice rasped from the small dog in Jake's hands. "We did as Veneswill bid. The Pitchborn is home."

"But, boss," Shadow said, touching noses with the terrier.

"Set me down, boy," Whisper ordered. Jake did as he was told.

"What are your orders?" Shadow asked, sitting down obediently. "We stand before the gate home. With the creature returned, I'm not sure how long it will remain open."

"Long enough to get what we're owed," Whisped said, closing her eyes. "Go find the emperor, Shadow. Tell him our business is finished."

"Aye, boss," Shadow said. "Best climb up top, boy," Shadow told Jake as he stood back up.

Jake pulled himself up on the beast, and the pair trotted into the madness as ably as a three-legged dog could bear.

Juniper

A song woke Juniper—Slow's song (though she didn't know it then). Her whole body hurt, and for a second, she didn't know where she was. It was dark and dirty, and she was lying on a big stone slab. And everywhere, she heard loud, ugly noise.

Except for the music.

Juniper suddenly wondered if that's what bluesmen's music sounded like on their guitars.

Slow! Juniper sat up at the thought of her new friend, and everything returned to her with a whooshing sound—the monsters, Mr. Jack, her grandma's ghost going into her grandma's body, all of it.

Juniper looked over to where Molly's body lay. Two beams connected to the Augment Glass fired into Molly, and a third hit Mr. Jack. Juniper watched Mr. Jack scream, rolling around in the mud from the pain.

Molly wasn't moving.

Juniper dashed through the distance between them and nudged Molly's shoulder.

"Molly?" Juniper cried. "Molly, wake up. Wake up!"

Molly did not answer.

"Molly," Juniper gently lifted Molly's head and cradled it in her lap, stroking her hair. "Grandma!"

Molly flinched but didn't wake.

Juniper kept stroking her grandmother's hair.

"Okay, okay, um," Juniper's eyes quickly took in the scene around her. Slow played his guitar on a small boulder as the monsters surrounded him. Tod was there—making Juniper wonder for a second if she was still asleep and if all this was a nightmare—running toward Slow. And all around them, that horrible humming sounded to Juniper like angry, growling toads in a swamp. It was their humming that made Juniper think of her mom's song.

"Mom used to sing a song to me at bedtime," Juniper began, returning her gaze to Molly's face. "She said it was an old melody that you taught her. It went like this—"

And Juniper leaned closer to her grandma's ears, humming her mom's song.

"Come on, you remember it, right? Wake up, Grandma! Wake up!"

Juniper kept humming anyhow.

The Pitch

Agares felt full for the first time in his recent memory. The dirge was causing immense pain, which translated to power for him. Soon, there would be no stopping him.

Not this time.

He returned his attention to the battlefield—if one wanted to use the term *battlefield* loosely. This was no battle, after all, but an execution—so many of his enemies in the same place at the same time. Having young Winslow join the board was a stroke of tremendous luck.

"It's a valiant effort, trying to play your music louder than mine," Agares spoke toward where Winslow had been standing before being surrounded by Pitchborn. "It's a shame to lose you. But you've outlived your usefulness, you understand."

Agares felt his power swell, and while it allowed him to spread more of himself into his Pitchborn army, strengthening his control over them, he wondered what caused the increase.

Until he saw Claptrap barreling across the field, dodging stones and fellow Pitchborn alike as he made his way toward his master.

"So, the budding psychopath and the mindless creature," Agares smiled. "I believe it's time we wrap things up now and be on our way."

Agares raised both arms, lifting the Augment Glass high as he brought his symphony of agony to one more crescendo before it finished off both of its victims.

"Two out of three ain't bad," he laughed. "I'll just mop up the girl after."

Slow

Slow could feel his fingers losing strength, but he kept playing, even as he dodged crazy nightmare creatures. He slipped once, smashing his shoulder into a large stone, but it never stopped his song.

The chanting of the creatures seemed to be quieting some if it wasn't Slow's imagination. Maybe those horrible home movies playing in the sky would stop soon, too.

A pot-bellied pig with a fish's face ran into Slow's feet, knocking him to the ground, and then Tod was on him. The boy who had attacked Slow, what now seemed like forever ago, hit pretty hard. The boy currently hitting Slow was bringing something else entirely to his punches. Slow felt a rib give, maybe two before he could deflect the next punch with Yvette. Then, he racked Tod with a well-placed kick, sending the boy to his knees. Slow got up before more Pitchborn came, unhooked his Pignose, and walloped Tod in the side of the head with it.

"That's for drowning me!" Slow said.

Nearby, Slow saw Agares bellow in rage and pain, dropping the Augment Glass.

The Pitchborn continued their guttural chanting, but before Slow could react to what looked like their master shaking off pain, Agares stood on top of the boulder before him, pointing at Slow.

"Pitchborn, heed me!" the man yelled. "Kill them all."

Molly

The next Molly knew she was lying in a familiar field. Only this visit to Edvard Grieg's song didn't find her wearing a dress, but her typical jeans and t-shirt outfit.

And there was no Calithan.

Molly stood up and looked around. The field was freshly mowed this time, and the treeline in the distance was clear of brush.

Was she dead? She didn't want that to be the case. But dying so that Juniper could live would be an easy trade. She really wanted, no, *needed* to know that her plan had worked, though.

"Calithan!" Molly yelled, looking for the besuited man in his tails. "Calithan, is Juniper okay? If I'm not dead—and I like Grieg just as much as the next girl, but I wouldn't call this much of an afterlife—I don't know how to get back. How do I get back to Juniper!"

Despite her worry and frustration mounting, Molly still couldn't keep her smile from coming. She hugged her arms around herself and breathed deeply through her nose, exhaling out her mouth.

I'm me.

In her moment of connecting to herself, Molly heard the song. Someone, somewhere in the distance, was humming a tune she recognized. She couldn't place it exactly at first, only that it was familiar.

When the memory hit Molly, she teared up.

But these wear happy tears—a healing cry.

When Alice had been four or five—Molly couldn't precisely remember which age—she'd gotten chicken pox and had to stay indoors until she healed. Little Alice Matheson hated nothing more than being stuck inside, not when there were forests to explore and adventures to be had. So, one day, Molly told her precocious daughter that the adventures would still be out there when she was feeling better but that they could make up a song to take her mind off things if she thought she was up to it.

Thus, *The Song of Wondering* was born.

Upon placing the tune, Molly began to remember and sing the lyrics she and her little girl had made up those many years ago.

> *If a star falls near, do you hear a boom?*
>
> *And can you tame ants living in your room?*
>
> *How do flowers pick their colored petals?*
>
> *And what do racers do with all their medals?*
>
> *I'm gonna make my Wondering List up wide,*
>
> *And find all the answers when I'm next outside!*

Sometimes, Molly would sing the first verse, and Alice would return the rhyming verse. Other times, Alice would go first. It was a simple tune that was a home for simple wonderings, and that was fine with them. They continued their Song of Wondering all of their days.

That Molly was hearing the tune now made her feel Alice with her, and then she realized that Calithan had been right before.

Grief isn't a book that you start, read to the end, and finish.

It's more like a song that gets stuck in your head, coming and going at will. Sometimes, you see or hear something that makes you start humming the tune, and it's in your head, unbidden. Other times, you sing the song outright, two or three times in a row, because you miss it. All the music of the world will come and go, and yet here's this song. So you make peace with it, acknowledging it when it comes with a nod. But remember, *it's not the only song.*

"That I now have a grief song doesn't mean I lose *The Wondering Song*," Molly said. To no one. To anyone—herself most of all.

"Okay, Alice," Molly said, controlling her breathing purposefully. "Let's go get your baby girl."

Molly focused on the humming, which caused it to grow louder, filling the field and forests around her, and began to sing along with it.

Then, the field stood empty.

*   *   *   *   *

Molly came to and found herself in Juniper's lap. She smiled up into her grandaughter's face, who was humming with her eyes closed, and then Molly continued singing *The Wondering Song*, getting to her feet. Juniper helped her grandma stand, and Molly smiled at the edge of her lips as her song grew louder.

Agares turned atop the boulder he was standing on and screamed at Molly before chanting again, trying to embolden his Pitchborn masses to drown out Molly's song.

Somewhere, out in the dark, a guitar started to play the most wondrous song. It wasn't Molly's song, *The Wondering Song*, but it accompanied her song beautifully until their combined musicality overtook Agares and his Pitchborn's death dirge.

Then Molly saw Jake Steadherd riding on top of what looked like a black mastiff through a sea of malformed monstrosities, and the ridiculousness almost made her laugh.

Juniper hopped off the dais suddenly, and everything that happened next seemed to happen in slow motion, yet all at once.

The Pitch

The rocky dreamscape that was The Pitch grew quiet, the final riff of Slow's guitar echoing off into the starless night. Molly panted, breathless on the dais as Slow tried to get some feeling into his fingers behind his boulder. Juniper looked to be running toward Jake as he and his mastiff steed bound some fifty feet away toward her.

And everywhere around them, monsters stood bleating, growling, or squawking, restlessly awaiting orders from their master.

Agares began to laugh, deep and loud. Slowly, at first, menacing. But it turned into what sounded like actual glee.

"Oh, that was a wonderful time," Agares said. "What fun! You dreamed up a final defense and bested my dirge. If only I didn't have this army here, ready to rip you limb from limb. But, alas, I've got places to be. Your world next, if you can believe it."

He turned, arms to his side, and bellowed so loudly it filled whatever the boundaries of The Pitch were.

"Pitchborn! Kill everything that is not us."

It was like a switch had been flipped, igniting every Pitchborn into a furious rage. A panda coated in slimy gray soup and the lower body of a serpent began to slither toward Molly as a dozen eyeballs with bat wings swarmed Slow.

Rodger, though, ran *toward* Claptrap.

"Give me my daughter!" Rodger screamed. An enraged father replaced the once pleasant wordsmith who befriended Juniper in Kings Park.

The citizens of Timberhaven—and those just visiting—faced their doom, surrounded by hundreds of creatures born of nightmares who would kill them.

Molly focused on the panda serpent, kicking and dodging as she could.

Rodger punched Claptrap, breaking long, spindly arms as the Pitchborn ripped and bit into him.

Slow swung his Pignose with abandon.

However, the entirety of Juniper's focus was on Jake, whose steed was riding toward Claptrap, even while Jake looked back at her. She slid into the mud and grabbed something.

"C'mon, Juniper," Jake yelled. "I know the way out—"

"I'm really, really sorry, Jake!" Juniper cried.

A toy Tesla coil that was ninety feet tall and thirty feet wide filled the sky above the battle scene. Given their familiarity with giant Pitchborn ordering them around, the Pitchborn paused to look up, and that caused everyone to stop for a moment.

Everyone except Jake, who jumped down off the back of Shadow and tried to hide.

"What is this madness?" Agares scoffed.

Then, the Tesla coil began to spin.

Belief is a powerful thing.

It can help the sick get well when they might not have otherwise.

It can see you through the hard times and to the other side.

But sometimes, it can keep you from shaking the thought that something will bring you pain, even when your best friend tells you it won't.

Jake *knew* those sparks in Juniper's toy would hurt if they hit you. He *believed* they were like fireballs.

And so they were.

Plumes of fire began to streak from the giant Tesla coil, showering all over The Pitch and crashing in small explosions. Pitchborn flew through the air far and wide as fires began to spread in the wake of the destruction.

Rodger used the distraction to get the jump on Claptrap, knocking the creature to the ground. In kicking the Pitchborn again, however, Rodger realized that Claptrap was just a dumb animal. Any blame that it had coming to it for his daughter's disappearance should really be placed on the one holding its leash. Rodger stopped his attack just as two dogs emerged from somewhere—one missing a leg and the other an eye—and started ripping into Claptrap.

Rodger watched as Agares uttered a guttural scream and fell from his perch atop the boulder. He started toward Agares but saw that Molly needed help fending off a few Pitchborn as she tried getting to her granddaughter.

No more lost little girls, he thought.

The surviving members of Agares' army began to run, fly, or slither for the hills to escape the tower of death that was Juniper's Tesla coil—his control over them utterly shattered.

Once the herd thinned out enough and the stragglers left weren't attacking, Juniper put her toy back in her hoodie, emptying the sky for the last time. Molly ran the final few feet to her grandchild and hugged her.

"Are you okay," Molly asked, her face every bit as dirty as Juniper's.

"I'm okay," Juniper replied.

"That was very clever, using the toy," Rodger said, putting a hand first on Juniper's shoulder and then Molly's.

At that, Juniper slid away and went to Jake, who was crying in a ball in the mud.

Juniper bent and sat with him, hugging Jake.

"I'm really sorry, Jake," Juniper offered as he hugged her back.

Rodger walked over and sat down in the mud with the pair, with Molly following suit.

"After I figured out how this worked," Juniper said, still holding the Augment Glass, "and I saw that Jake was here, I knew what to do. But I also knew it would scare Jake really bad."

Rodger took the Augment Glass and looked it over.

"Sounds to me like it took the both of you to save us from the monsters," Molly offered.

"That's exactly what I was thinking," Rodger agreed. "We've got a couple of real heroes here."

Jake looked up, his eyes wet, and wiped his nose on his bloody shirt. He smiled, but he kept an arm around Juniper.

"Everyone okay?"

"Slow!" Juniper hopped up and ran over to the teen, wrapping him in a hug. Jake was quick behind her and did the same.

Slow hugged both kids back, ensuring his guitar didn't hit either.

Molly walked over. "It feels like we already know each other."

Slow offered his hand to shake. "It does, ma'am. But officially, my name's Winslow."

"But his friends call him Slow," Juniper added.

Molly ignored his hand and hugged him.

*   *   *   *   *

Agares had reverted to his true form of an inch-tall crocodile with hawk wings and crawl-hopped over to Tod's body, slowly, ever so slowly. He told himself it was because he needed to keep quiet and not attract the attention of his enemies during their lovefest, but he also knew the truth.

He was too weak to do otherwise.

As Agares reached him, his unconscious lackey began to stir.

"What is—"

No, Agares thought, hopping upon Tod's face. Tod grunted, trying to shake him off, but quickly went still. *I need back the power I used on you. I may be forced to leave without my army, but I'm still leaving.*

Agares began to grow, once again shedding his true form for the build of a human, taking on a different look than he'd had as *Collin*.

So be it, Agares thought as he walked toward the remaining gate out of his world and into another.

*   *   *   *   *

"Wake up," Veneswill's tiny voice shouted in Whisper's face. "Wake up, you worthless dog!"

Whisper, who'd just had a paw on the rainbow bridge and was about to cross before being rudely called back, opened her eyes.

"Agares is coming," the baby's face on Veneswill's trunk screamed. "He's changed forms. Hold him at bay until help arrives to dispose of him. Do so now—I command it!"

"We've not yet seen recompense for our previous dealings," Whisper could hardly get the words out.

"I care not!" Veneswill screeched in his mosquito-buzzing voice, hopping angrily and slapping Whisper's nose with his worm-like snout. "I want—"

Whisper used the last of her life force to gobble the tiny Pitchborn up and then died, having swallowed The Emperor of Refuse.

All was quiet as Agares of The Pitch, recent escapee of The Hollows of Nil, walked through the gate and into Timberhaven.

*   *   *   *   *

Juniper screamed, and everyone spun to see why.

Tod walked from behind the boulder in a daze, utterly unreacative to Juniper. His eyes were glassy, and he stutter stepped as he walked in a lazy shuffle.

"What's your name, boy?" Rodger asked with his arms up, prepared to fight.

"Tod?" Jake asked, slowly walking over to his brother.

"Careful, Jake," Juniper said.

Tod's head tilted at his little brother, but not with any recognition. To Tod, there was just a tiny person in front of him where there hadn't been before.

Two dogs appeared protectively on either side of Jake and growled at his brother.

"I think it's okay, guys," Jake said. He took Tod's big hand in his little one and guided his brother away from the boulder. "But we should probably go home now."

Thanks to Jake and his dogs, the wild crew made their way toward the gate home.

"Oh, this is yours, Mr. Jack—er, I mean Rodger," Juniper said. She pulled his hat from her hoodie and handed it to him.

"I wondered if you might be willing to trade," Rodger said, still examining the Augment Glass as they walked.

"Oh no!" Jake yelled. He dropped Tod's hand and ran toward a tunnel of green energy roughly three feet high. But then he pulled to the side of it.

He and the other two dogs knelt at the side of another dog.

"I'm sorry, Jake," Molly said, patting Jake's back.

"Looks like we better hurry, all," Rodger said. "This gate is shrinking fast."

"We've got to take her back to Timberhaven," Jake said. "She didn't want to die here."

The mastiff gathered the small dog in its massive maw, and then all three dogs went through the gate, leaving the party behind.

Jake gathered Tod's hand again and helped him kneel into a crawl. "Okay, we can go now."

"Let's go home," Molly said, hugging Juniper from behind while they waited for the Steadherd brothers to clear the ever-diminishing gate.

"I think this is where I say goodbye," Rodger said.

"What?" Juniper said.

"Rodger, are you sure?" Molly asked, seemingly not surprised.

Rodger nodded. "I am. I think I can use the Augment Glass to find Melinda. She's somewhere over here. I can feel it."

Juniper hugged him around the waist.

"Hey, it's going to be okay now," Rodger said, kneeling before the little girl. "You'll see. And thank you so much for being such a good friend to your ol' Mr. Jack. I'm not sure I would have made it without you."

Juniper just nodded, still hugging him.

"I'll be in touch," Rodger told Molly.

"We'll wait to hear from you," Molly nodded. "Come along now, Juniper."

Juniper joined her grandma as the two began to crawl through the gate. When they reached the other side, sitting in the grass of Kings Park at nighttime, Juniper yelled back through, "If you don't keep me, I break. What am I?"

The gate shrunk to the size of a basketball, but just as it disappeared further, Juniper heard Mr. Jack laugh and answer, "A promise! I'll see you again, Juniper Soot!"

And then the gate closed.

Timberhaven

Had either the sheriff hunting Tod Steadherd or the trio of women from The Pub been a mere five minutes earlier, they would have all seen a strange man blink into existence in Kings Park, and everything that would happen in Timberhaven in the months ahead might not have come to pass. But Fate plays as it will, and they weren't there. The man was left to escape The Pitch and slink into the dark forest to tend to his plotting unhindered.

But this is a tale for another time.

$$* \quad * \quad * \quad * \quad *$$

"And I'm telling you, Nickie," Brynne repeated, hurrying them along, "I don't know what we'll be looking at when we get to the park, but your help is needed."

"I should have brought my bag, is all I'm saying," Nickie sighed. This evening had been insane already.

Sheriff Vindego's cruiser's siren chirped as he pulled up behind them, walking along the side of the road.

"You ladies alright?" he asked.

"Officer, yes, no," Essa began, then saw the two boys in the back of the police car. "You look to have been busy already this night. But no, we could use your help. You see—"

The sheriff grabbed his radio, and his voice exploded from the speakers on his cruiser. "Tod Steadherd, not another step. You stop right there. Get on the ground!"

His car sped past the women and skidded at the edge of Kings Park, right in front of a strange cast of dirty, beat-up characters: Molly and her granddaughter and the Steadherd boys. Tod's little brother was trying to coax him onto the ground.

"Brock, wait just a second," Brynne stopped, taking the sheriff by the arm as the other two women walked on. "Now, you can find out with us what's going on here, or you can chalk this up to an Old Town incident and leave it at that. Your call."

"Brynne, I've already got these two idiots on the destruction of property out at Molly's place —at the least—and

372

they don't do anything without that psycho," Brock said, pointing at Tod, who, admittedly, looked to Brock like he was on something and not his typical charming self.

"Sheriff, call a rig down," Nickie called from over in the park. She had been looking everyone over and was now paying close attention to Tod. "Better find this boy's parents, too."

*   *   *   *   *

Story, the brown tabby (but much more, as you've no doubt figured out) wanted very badly to go to Juniper but walked down the sidewalk away from Kings Park, trekking up until she reached the fountain outside The Pub. She hopped up on the fountain's edge and paced a bit before stepping behind Timberhaven and into Calithan's bar.

The bar was empty save for two people: a thin, wispy creature at the bar and a young woman seated at an otherwise empty table. Story walked five feet toward the bar and hopped up toward the tender.

"Duraine. I assume Calithan's waiting for me?" Story said, purring.

"Yes, ma'am," Duraine said, a quick head bow in respect. "He'll be down presently."

"Never seen this one so polite," Twist said from the table. "Quite a sight."

When Story turned her back, Duraine stuck her tongue out at the cello player.

"You're the sprite of Slow's grandmother," Story said more than she asked. "He is quite heroic, your grandson."

Twist visibly relaxed at the news that Slow had made it through the Niksik, then gathered her composure.

"He doesn't know," Twist said. "Who I am, I mean. We never got around to none of that. Wasn't time."

Story nodded. "Just the same, I'll see that Calithan squares the favor he owes."

"Already done, ma'am," Duraine said from behind the cat.

Twist gave the tender a confused yet grateful head bow.

"*We need the room, ladies,*" Calthan's voice came from the stairs nearby. Both Duraine and Twist gathered to leave. Twist gave a nod of respect to Story, similar to Duraine's.

"Copycat," Duraine said, bumping Twist's leg as the two left. "No disrespect meant!" the tender called over her shoulder to Story.

Calithan waved his hand, and all the pathways into the bar, visible and not, were sealed off and locked.

"*We're beyond prying eyes,*" Calithan said. "*Excepting the Witnesses, of course.*"

Story walked down the bar closer to its owner anyway.

"As you've no doubt realized, my trip bore fruit," Story said.

"*All of this could be far more easily handled if your brother didn't keep his cards so close to his metaphorical vest,*" Calithan scoffed.

"Mystery does as he will, as do I, the same as ever," Story said.

"*The rumors are true, then*," Calithan said. "*He and his companion are coming to Timberhaven.*"

"Three times," Story said, her cat eyes narrowing. "The first time as help. The second as harm."

"*And the third*?" Calithan asked.

"That will depend on you and the councils," Story said. "But you *must* keep Juniper out of it. All of it. Everything is happening sooner this time. I'd only just gotten back from my fact-finding. I hadn't rested enough to guide her properly. If Jake hadn't seen the Pitchborn…"

"*Things must have been bad for you to have needed my aid with Molly. I didn't realize*," Calithan said in the way of apology. "*And Agares almost finished Juniper in The Pitch, I hear. Your girl is very clever to have survived on her own.*"

"She *wasn't* alone," Story said, hopping off the bar. "And ensuring that she stays that way is a key to winning the battle ahead."

House of

Healing

Home

Molly sat at her kitchen table, listening to the sounds of her house. It was as if the collected nails, boards, and concrete had a pulse again for the first time in ages.

They'd come home from the hospital last night to the shattered glass and broken back door but had been too tired to do anything about them. A phone call woke Molly in the morning, and she then came downstairs to find a now blonde-haired Audrey Fell clearing the broken glass in the kitchen while Wesley Bells worked on repairing the back door. Someone had even called Elbert Chessman and lined him up to fix Molly's broken bay window.

The children ran down the stairs just behind Molly. Both were still in clothes from the hospital gift shop, but now Juniper was wearing Mr. Jack's purple bowler hat. Slow, who'd crashed on the couch, sat up and stretched, testing the hospital wrap around his ribs.

"Careful, now, you guys," Audrey told Juniper and Jake while the two walked to join Slow in the living room. "Molly, just have a seat. Wesley is nearly done fixing your door, and then I'll get some breakfast started once the glass is cleaned up. What's everyone hungry for?"

"Anything's good!" Jake said, beaming a smile.

"Not tuna casserole, please," Molly added, catching her granddaughter's eyes and smiling. Juniper smiled back.

"I like tuna casserole," Jake said.

"You haven't been eating it forever," Juniper told him.

Soon, the house filled with the sound of eggs frying and the smells of fresh coffee and cooked bacon. Audrey laughed at Jake's reaction to so much fresh fruit as he ate a banana, an apple, then an orange. Wesley juggled hot biscuits from the oven as the kids watched, mesmerized, and then Slow taught Juniper how to build the perfect egg sandwich. Even Elbert joined them at the breakfast table, at Molly's insistence, once the new window was in place.

"I've got the dishes," Slow announced, standing and gathering empty plates and silverware.

"Me, too," Jake shouted and picked up his glass. It still had a little apple juice, so he hurriedly drank it.

"Nope, not today," Audrey said, waving both boys down to be seated. "Wesley and I've got this. Besides, someone has a birthday gift to unwrap."

Juniper stood next to Molly, who pulled her in close. With her grandma still seated, the two looked eye-to-eye.

"I'm very sorry to have missed your birthday," Molly said. "We don't do that in this house—birthdays are a big deal. And we will have a make-up party, you better believe."

"Can I come?" Jake asked, standing next to Molly, too.

"Duh," Juniper smiled. "If you don't come, I won't have any friends there."

"I'll come," Audrey said.

"Me, too," Wesley added.

Molly released Juniper and pulled Jake onto her lap. She then put her arm back around her granddaughter, holding both children.

"Jake," Molly said quietly. "Juniper. I wondered if I could talk to both of you about something before we get to the present."

Jake put his head on Molly's chest, listening to her heartbeat, suddenly overwhelmed at the physical touch.

"The sheriff called me this morning," Molly said.

Audrey nodded her head toward the living room at Wesley and Slow. "Hey, Slow, I wondered if you could introduce me, Mr. Chessman, and Wesley to Yvette."

Soon, it was just Molly, Juniper, and Jake in the kitchen. Juniper started breathing heavier. The morning had gone too well, and something terrible was about to happen.

"It's okay," Molly said, patting Juniper's back. "Well, it could be okay. That's really up to you two."

"More monsters?" Jake asked, lifting his head.

"No, just a choice is all," Molly said. "See, Jake, your mom, she has to go on a trip right now. And she's not sure when she'll be back."

Per Molly's phone call from the sheriff that morning, the truth was that Denise Steadherd packed her few belongings into a borrowed Chevy and left town. It seemed that Tod, the son she doted on, was broken, maybe beyond repair, and she didn't have any mothering left in her for Jake.

"And since your brother is in the hospital getting well," Molly continued. "If it's okay with Juniper, I wanted to see how you felt about staying here with us."

Juniper's breath caught in her chest like it could not get past the happiness in her heart at the idea of a new family. "I say okay. It'll be fun, Jake!"

"I can live here?" Jake asked.

Molly took the tight, crying hug the little boy gave her as a Yes.

*　*　*　*　*

It was a great morning that became a great day—as if the night before hadn't been filled with monsters and madness at all.

Mr. Chessman left first.

Audrey and Wesley stayed a bit longer, helping Juniper set up her new telescope in the attic at a beautiful spot right by the window. Jake helped until Wesley asked him what he knew about fairytales. Once they left, the telescope got set up much faster.

At one point, Slow and Molly were in the living room, talking and enjoying the small fire in the fireplace. October was getting colder now, and Molly's house was all the cozier for it.

Slow noticed the painting on the wall of a black woman singing from atop a piano and got up to inspect it.

"Who's this?" he asked, stirring his mug of hot apple cider with a cinnamon stick.

"Ah," Molly said, standing with him. "I painted that years ago. That's Trish 'Twist' Mulligan. A jazz singer who meant a lot to me when I was about your age."

Slow's hands began to shake so much he had to put his mug down.

"No way," he said, looking closer at the painting. He couldn't be sure. It seemed Molly was a gifted painter, but she hadn't been going for realism in the piece. "Did she play the cello?"

Molly looked at him wide-eyed.

"She's much younger here—before she was married," Slow said, his eyes getting misty. "But that's Patricia Perkins. She's the one who led me to Timberhaven to find the magic music. That's my grandma."

Molly hugged the bluesman as the two laughed at the absurd wonder of it all until finally, Slow broke the hug.

"Can I use your phone? I'd like to talk to my folks."

The village of Timberhaven
October 31, 2009
Halloween

"I'll be right here afterward, and then we go trick-or-treating for real, capisce?" Molly said, unlocking the doors to her car.

"Capisce!" Jake yelled and opened his door. He wore a white shirt and brown vest, and a cardboard sword was hanging from his rope belt with little strands of ivy placed throughout the vest and belt.

"We'll come straight back here," Juniper agreed. Her long brown hair was tucked under a black wig, and Molly had drawn a pencil mustache above her lip that was much better than the stick-on mustache. Juniper looked like a dapper young man in the 1920s in her little black suit jacket. She fidgeted with the Tesla coil in her pocket but was careful to keep it out of sight of Jake. He was still a little nervous around the toy.

"Grandma?" Juniper hesitated before opening her door. She watched as Jake showed some other kids his handful of beans. "Thank you."

"You got it, love," Molly smiled through the rearview mirror. "Now, it's All Hallow's Eve. Go show this school how we Mathesons and Soots party!"

Juniper smiled and climbed out of the car. She waved back to her grandma before catching up to Jake and entering the school party.

*   *   *   *   *

Juniper sat alone on the bleachers, watching the other children go from table to table, dressed as Spider-Man and Batman, pirates, witches, and princesses, collecting candy from the teachers and entering the homemade funhouse the school had set up in the gymnasium.

She touched Slow's letter, what he'd called his "see you later" letter, in her pocket. They'd all said their goodbyes before he headed back home to his family, but Slow said he wanted Juniper to have something to keep in her lab from him, which did bring her some comfort.

However, the letter still had never left Juniper's pocket.

Jake was having a blast, telling everyone he was Jack the Giant Slayer and showing off his sword and magic beans. It was as if he was a different boy once he was out from underneath Tod's harmful gaze, and the other children flocked to him.

But nobody knew who Nikola Tesla was—not even any of Juniper's teachers.

Juniper couldn't decide if that bothered her or not. Scientists often had a tough time being scientists, from what she understood. Not being known, except by other scientists, was probably part of *being* a scientist, for all she knew.

"That's her," Jake's voice snapped Juniper out of her thoughts. "She's my best friend, and she's a scientist."

Jake led a little black girl dressed in a long white lab coat and oversized glasses to where Juniper sat. The girl was a little taller than Jake, about Juniper's height.

"Hey, Juniper," Jake announced with a wave from the bottom bleachers. "This is Maya. She's a—" he turned back to the girl following him. "What are you dressed as again?"

"An aerospace engineer," Maya explained.

"She's an airspace musketeer!" Jake shouted up to Juniper. "I told her you're a scientist that has a spark coil but don't show her 'til I leave, okay?"

Juniper stood up as the pair approached, looking over Maya's costume as the new girl looked over hers. Maya wore a nametag that read *M. Jackson*.

"Mary Jackson?" Juniper guessed.

"Nikola Tesla?" Maya guessed back.

The pair blinked, shook hands like they were grown-ups, and then fell about in giggles, happy to know another scientist.

Look for Juniper and her friends next in

Secrets in the Library!

Author's Note

Twelve years ago, I started a book while participating in a writing challenge. I only knew two things about this book: I wanted it to take place around Halloween, and I wanted to expand on Juniper Soot, a character I'd made up for my wife Lauren's birthday story once upon a time.

Monsters in the Park is what came out of the deal.

While it started quickly at first, pouring out of me like I was merely dictating actual events from the realm of imagination, that speed eventually ebbed. Timberhaven, you see, is my pondering place. Sure, big, fantastical things happen there, but it's at the pace of a country summer when you're twelve—slow and leisurely whether you like it or not. Ideas and relationships within the small town of Timberhaven take time to work themselves and each other out.

Plus, the real world became an all too real factor.

Seven years into writing this, my mom began to exhibit signs of Alzheimer's.

Eight years in, we saw a worldwide pandemic, which made the artist in me want to step away from Timberhaven and focus on creating lighter adventures and comic books.

Nine years in, we lost my father-in-law.

Two months after that, my dad.

Juniper was always a kid who had come to live with her grandma after a loss, but when I dreamt her up for my wife, neither of us knew what it was like to lose a parent. Molly came into this story suffering from memory issues born of Timberhaven, but she was, regardless, a woman dealing with confusion and lost time. Eventually, these became things that were too harsh a thread for this author to pick at as I followed the story to its end.

But here we are. I finally got to a place where I could tell Juniper's story. Jake's. Slow, Molly, and Rodger's.

Timberhaven's story.

Thanks for discovering this found family with me. I hope you enjoyed it and will return as I continue The

Timberhaven Chronicles. The saga is unfolding much more quickly for me now. If you can't wait for their next book, you can find Jake, Juniper, and her new friend Maya in my other published Timberhaven works—*Before the Weaver* has two Juniper and Jake tales that take before this novel chronologically, and all three kids share a scene in *Waking the Weaver*, which takes place after.

Until next time,

A.C.

A special shout out to Scott and Joy Miller for introducing Timberhaven to Nickie Fraser.

And to Dusty Dean, Juniper Soot's biggest champion, second only to my wife.

www.ingramcontent.com/pod-product-compliance
Lightning Source LLC
Chambersburg PA
CBHW050917030726
47503CB00007BB/2342